The Cut Off

Mark James Montgomery

THE CUT OFF
First Hardback Edition, August, 2022
Copyright 2022 Mark James Montgomery
STON3HOUSE
ISBN: 978-1-0878-5386-4

For those who have a compass and get lost anyway

Chapter 1

He arrives late for the memorial, the bright Southern California afternoon clashing with the aftermath of a burial. Mourners have collected in the backyard. They are dressed somberly, though the sunlight is playful, sparkling on wine glasses and silverware, discreet conversations held beneath a sky so blue and boundless it promises life eternal. It is a day of disunion, the deceased freshly committed to the claustrophobic embrace of the earth, the living gathered gratefully, even happily, on the firmament above.

The airy, empyrean atmosphere of Mr. Jackson Cantwell's final reception is reflected in the bronzed lenses of Mrs. Cantwell's sunglasses. Not entirely bereaved, she sits at an outdoor table sipping from her glass of pinot grigio as she watches her son make his surefooted way across the clipped lawn. He is tall, slender, with his father's breadth of shoulder and a brooding aspect Mrs. Cantwell is certain was also handed down from his father, her own bearing regal and tirelessly businesslike. Her hand goes out to him and Cole Cantwell grasps it, sliding into a chair across from her.

"Thank you for coming all this way," Mrs. Cantwell says.

He presses her palm. "It's nothing. What can I do here?"

Cole Cantwell is thirty, wears a white dress shirt and dark sport coat, items he'd scrambled to come up with for the occasion. The drive down had removed him from his own domestic crisis in the Bay Area, a chilly stand-off with a live-in girlfriend, then five-hundred miles of steaming traffic that triggered a few outbursts in the confines of his car and caused him to miss the proceedings at the cemetery. Hurrying through the shady and deserted silence, he cursed himself on finding his father's grave neatly filled.

Mrs. Cantwell's lenses are fixed on her son, dispassionate, judicious. "If your schedule permits it, what you could do, dear, is help Paul clear out the garage. It hasn't been possible to enter it for years."

Cole's own sunglasses don't quite conceal his negative reaction. He doesn't hate Paul, but he dislikes the idea of him mightily, as well as his mother's loss of discernment for taking up with him. His father did leave her in the lurch, off on one of his unfeasible pursuits, on that last occasion a simpler life in a palapa on the Sea of Cortez, but Paul was a second-rater in all respects, a very poor stand-in for the swashbuckling Jackson Cantwell. For all his faults, and they were manifold, Cole's father channeled electricity, he pulsed with life, even during his absences as a family man.

Cole says, "Paul's back in the picture?"

A well-wisher momentarily interrupts them, stopping by to offer his condolences. Mrs. Cantwell responds without words, but graciously, then returns to her son.

"I'll consort with whomever I choose, Cole."

"That's dad's stuff in there," he says. It sounds dim-witted. Of course it was his dad's stuff in there, a moldering storehouse of things Jackson Cantwell had ceased to use – his golf clubs, his tennis racket, his shotgun for clay pigeons, rusting away. His documents, without context, his photographs of old friends and times, now brittle pages of ghosts. A man's memorial. It should have been valuable, but in the here and now, it seems to have no value at all.

His mother coolly sums it up. "In terms of dad's stuff, the mice have gotten to it."

Cole squints over the lawn. His father never deluded himself. He knew who and what he was and when his heart attack laid him out he faced the facts. He ditched his beachcomber's life and made it back to a cardiac clinic in San Bernardino. He'd suffered a Left Anterior Descending Occlusion, otherwise known as The Widowmaker, which didn't occur then but did in due time. He'd lost a sizable portion of heart muscle, his charm, his heft, and he didn't welcome Cole's few pilgrimages to his barren hospital room. The place smelled like death. Cole demanded his mother allow her errant husband to die at home. Jack Cantwell refused it. He wanted to spare her his gasping conclusion and it was one of the few hard turns he ever spared her.

For Cole's part, he wasn't present when his father raggedly

breathed his conclusion, he was in that indeterminate elsewhere he'd constructed for himself, a nebulous station between the last place and the next. Missing the funeral services, the mourners' long faces, his father's coffin being lowered into a rectangle in the grass, was not entirely unexpected by those present.

Reception-goers fade in and out of Cole's view. There are lots of Jackson Cantwell's associates in attendance. His father was willful and unapologetic and not everyone is haunted by the occasion. Cole spots one of them now.

"Some bald fucker just passed by smirking," he says.

Mrs. Cantwell, forbearing him, finishes her wine, gracefully resting the glass.

"It's just us now," her son reminds her. "Last of the line."

"Unless you and Sandra come up with something."

"You don't sound that hopeful."

Her gaze pierces him. "Should I be?"

Cole gives no answer. He is getting restless. He sees that his afternoon here will be a long one, with no real purpose, and his mother sees it too. A familiar barrier exists between them. Each has witnessed the others' misbehavior and forgiveness among the Cantwells is not freely dispensed.

"I think probably I'll head out first thing in the morning," Cole says. "We can handle the garage later."

Mrs. Cantwell merely watches him. He hates to ask her for anything, but his needle is on empty, he is running on fumes.

"I got caught a little short. Can you extend a small loan?"

His mother smiles, a nice white smile, pats his hand.

"You know, honey," she says. "You never made much distance from the proverbial tree."

*

Highway 395 runs north-south through most of California along the eastern side of the Sierra Nevada range. Cole, determined to escape the roads he'd been mired in west of the mountains, chooses this route for his return to the Bay Area. The unfettered highway speaks to his soul – steep, snowy granite peaks towering to his left, the solitary high-desert rolling by on his right. After leaving the swarms of L.A. behind, everything up this way is clean and rugged. Authentic. Traffic is sparse, he feels renewed, maybe even redeemed. Until he comes in range of a phone tower and tries Sandra again, and gets her.

She picks up knowing it is Cole, but she still answers with a stock hello, and that's irritating – like she's getting into the practice of keeping distance between them.

"I've been trying to reach you," Cole tells her.

She responds too casually. "I've been busy." That just sort of hangs there, so she adds, "How did it go?"

"It's over. He's in the ground."

Cole is driving below some very jagged crowns, staring up from his open window. He sees the sky gliding in, storm-blue. A warning. He'd planned on running north to Reno, then heading west over Donner Pass, dropping down toward the Bay Area. Now the possibility of difficult weather has arisen. In his favor, he knows his way around, and the highway west over the mountains is well-traveled and plowed.

"I'm sorry," Sandra says. The signal, her voice, is wobbly. "About your dad."

Cole watches cloud shadow fall over the land ahead. "Don't be. His specialty was skipping out. This was his last exit."

"Like father, like son."

That pricks him. Sandra is very able with the pins. "Damn. You and my mother must have gotten together."

Sandra's response is lost to the airwaves.

Up ahead, a gas station is coming up. As Cole pulls into it, he sees it is abandoned. He skids to a stop, jumps out of the car with his phone. He holds it up, trying positions until Sandra's voice comes in.

"… can't do this anymore," she is saying.

"Sandra, this is not great timing."

"… lack of … Always running away. When things get –"

"*Sandra –*"

" – you're not fucking there."

"That's not true." He is getting heated. He manages his tone. "Why don't you hang in? I'm five hours out, heading over the pass."

He doesn't hear her. "You know how I feel about you."

"You can't even say it."

"Say what?" Cole asks. He knows what. An expression of fidelity. The Three Words. He imagines Sandra in the apartment, at the window, maybe watching a Lyft pull up below. It is probably raining, she'll have her hooded jacket on. Smooth and tight. The one she looks so damn good in.

Her voice comes in. "… ask you something. Do you have your skis in the back?"

In reflex, Cole turns to his car. A Suburu turbo wagon. Kind of a hot rod. It has 217,000 miles on it and every mile shows. In some ways, it is a glassed-in diorama of his lifestyle, his personality: a radar detector for fast road work, a gym bag with some dirty clothes, a speeding ticket from on the way down, a plastic bag of oranges bought from a dark little man on a median strip in West Covina, a paperback Sandra had urged on him that he would never get through – *How to Make a Plant Love You.* All in all, an interior littered with the unfinished and what was finished long ago. And yes, there are a pair of light weight, very swift Swiss-made skis in the back. He likes to get out in the backcountry and just push it, plunder the powder, take on big air. It works out the aggression, focuses it, cliff dropping the steep side.

"Those skis," Cole says to Sandra. "are grounded." Though he knows of a few prime backcountry resorts on the route over the pass and regrets he won't have time for an overnighter.

Wind gusts from the open range beyond, scattering sand across bleak concrete. Cole angles his phone. "Sandra? You there?"

"Sorry," she says before he loses her. "But I'm really not."

The image of their little apartment slides back to him, Sandra shouldering her travel bag, exiting the front door, closing it on the life they shared.

Cole stands in the wind, the phone to his ear, the line dead.

He stares out from under the gas station canopy, past an island where gas pumps once stood. The place is forsaken. As if to reinforce it, a tumbleweed somersaults across the lot.

He watches it bounce across the highway, explode against the bumper of an 18 wheeler grinding past.

*

A hard gust buffets Cole's car, he smells the coming snow. He has shot northward, filled the tank in Reno, turned west, climbed the grades of Highway 80 at a good clip, mud and ice banging the floorboards. Approaching Donner Summit, traffic abruptly bogs down, standing motionless as far as he can see.

Anxiety gnaws him, getting back in time to head Sandra off is at risk. He knows of a side road ahead that will take him to Donner Pass Road, the historic alternate route down the mountain. The Pass Road will likely also be plowed, he's used it many a winter on his cross-country jaunts, and it swings back into Highway 80. With luck, at that junction he'll be out ahead of the crowd and flying down the foothills toward the East Bay.

Inching toward the side road consumes some time and when Cole veers onto it the paving is buried. There is no turning back, his wagon dragging through snow to the wheel hubs. Icy rubble sheers the belly of the car, crushes against the suspension. The situation calls for a steady pace and the Suburu has never let him down. It's a champ, a mountain goat, the thing eats winter, you can not kill it.

The day darkens, snow billowing, visibility a gray haze. Up ahead, half a dozen vehicles have pulled to the side. They've opted to go no further. Cole's Suburu chugs past them.

He makes it another mile. The laden wipers struggle, the world gone white.

The tail lights of a pickup flare, the tailgate fast approaching from the tumbling snowfall. Tires churning, the rear sliding, the truck spins. Cole taps his brakes, watches the pickup glide backward into a high drift.

A man and woman stare out at him from the cave of the cab

as he passes. He can do nothing for them, he is trying to keep his own car planted.

Further on, he finds himself in the full blindness of a blizzard, the sky zinc, everything that descends from it. The trees are gone, the road. He has the steering wheel cranked, knows he's losing the car. He is involved in his own slide now, brakes juddering, and the Suburu slowly revolves, swinging to a banging stop nose-first against something hard, unmoving. He is thrown into his seatbelt, a web of crazed glass bursting across the windshield. The engine quits. Snow cascades.

Cole groans. The airbags have not deployed, they'd gone bad some time ago, and he is thankful he at least hasn't been punched in the face by a big bag of gas-filled nylon. He unsnaps the seatbelt, pushes his door open, reels out. The car is up against the trunk of a sturdy cedar, snow-loaded boughs tented over the hood. Silvery sleet sheets down, throwing a heavy blanket over all that is.

He glimpses something standing above him, on the buried grade of the road. He pushes through the snow toward it, makes out a road sign. Through the streaking snow, he learns that a hamlet he'd never heard of is not far off. The sign reads:

Cope
Elevation 7056
Population 200

Cole wades back to the car. In the stinging cold, he zips his jacket tight, finds his gloves. He snugs on a knit hat, opens the rear hatch, throws out his backpack, his skis, poles. He sits on the bumper, snaps on a pair of lime green boots. Arranging the skis, he settles the boots into the bindings. He slings his backpack on, slams the hatch lid. Using the poles, he pushes his way up to the grade.

His heels rise off the skis as he slides ahead, shrouded by snow, vanishing toward the hamlet of Cope.

Chapter 2

The blizzard blows through the afternoon. It is hard going, everything buried. Twice he angles off the hidden grade of the road and punches down into soft drifts. He collects much powder, icy in his clothes, his head and shoulders laden. The day wanes, he struggles to stay upright, and bend after bend in the road, the hamlet of Cope fails to appear.

The road ascends and leaves him climbing, pushing his skis and jabbing his poles, and this seems to go on endlessly. He is running out of reserves, but the snowfall has eased and he has fair visibility. He uses a granite ledge some distance away as a marker, his breath misting as he lurches his way forward. The deep shadows of twilight lengthen, then the peaks ringing him slide into darkness. The snow is bright enough to stay on track. Finally, as he rounds the granite ledge he'd sighted, a settlement appears.

Entering Cope, Cole plugs along a wide, tire-tracked street with snowy structures lining each side. Old buildings, some ramshackle, low dwellings, a gas station, a century-old two-story market of brick, all shuttered. Windows and doorways are dark. He sees not a single light anywhere, wonders if the place has been left to the freeze. The few vehicles parked along the street are white mounds. His skis break the silence, he is the only thing that moves.

He is cold, body-core cold, he needs to get out of the weather soon or his heart and brain will shut down. A wooden church with snow folded over the roof appears. The cross over the porch tilts left but it might do for shelter.

He passes a sign in the yard, *Church is Open Welcome,* then his boots clump loudly on the porch steps and he stands before the front door. It is pinewood, skinned of paint. Cole removes a glove, finds his penlight, lights up the door handle, burnished by decades of hands. The church looks and feels vacant and he thinks about the best way to breach the lock. He decides to slip in the blade of his Swiss Army, lever it against the latchbolt, and hope a deadbolt doesn't come into the picture.

He is forcing a frozen hand into his pocket for the knife when a voice on the other side of the door speaks out.

"Yes ?"

Cole's teeth clatter. His tongue is thick when using it.

"Hello. I'm Cole. Hiked in. Car went off the road."

There is silence behind the door.

"Know of a room? Place I can stay for the night?"

The silence continues.

"Doesn't have to be much. Some space on the floor…"

The voice is muted. "Why did you come here?"

Cole shivers mightily. "Sign says Church Open. Welcome."

"Does the church look open?"

Cole's breath smokes. "Sir, I am freezing out here."

More silence. Then the door handle shakes. The door opens a foot. A beam snaps on, probing Cole's features. He blinks into it.

The voice behind the beam sounds resigned.

"Enter."

*

The man who admits Cole is the Pastor of the church, though Cole is unsure if the church is still a going concern. In the stale gloom, they pass down a hallway, the flashlight leading.

"I have a cot near the furnace," the Pastor tells him.

Cole follows the Pastor, a wiry figure, dark to him until he turns and the light catches his face. Beard stubble, glasses. Eyes spectral. A thousand mea culpas confessed. "Do not ask me for a meal," he warns. "I have no provisions."

"Done." Cole rasps. "No meal."

They move down a narrow flight of groaning steps and enter a small basement, where, as the Pastor said, a cot waits near a furnace. The furnace is an ancient one, the low roar of heat heard through the ducting, flames jetting behind vents. Dim firelight plays through shadows draped with spiderwebs.

"There's a blanket on the cot," the Pastor says in leaving.

"Can I ask a question?" Cole inquires, wrestling off his backpack. "What's with this town? Why are all the lights off?"

The Pastor continues up the stairs.

Cole stares after him, stripping off his remaining frigid glove. He brings himself close to the furnace, drinking in the heat. The flames roar softly, his eyes close and his heart pulses.

The stairs groan again and he looks toward them. The Pastor is coming back down. He holds something. Leaning forward, he places it on the bottom step.

"You'll find tools on the shelf. I trust you can open this."

He turns, recedes.

Cole's gaze is fastened on the bottom step.

A can of chili has been offered. Cold. No spoon.

He makes short work of it

*

Cole Cantwell awakes in the gray light cutting through a narrow window well. He is on the cot, wrapped in the woolen blanket and he has been dreaming. An unsettling dream, one that involves something small and weighty watching him from the shadows. It has multiple eyes and as Cole stares overhead, his dream becomes real.

A fat spider is motionless in its strands of silk. It feeds on a smaller spider, its mandibles sucking the life from it.

Cole jerks upright, tosses the blanket, searching the gloom.

"Where's my fucking pack?"

He finds the Pastor in his office, shabby quarters with a wall-furnace creased with rust. He is at a desk piled with paperwork, periodicals, assorted household items – a box of cereal, a spray bottle of window cleaner.

Cole has stopped in the doorway. The Pastor, peering down at a book, gives him no glance.

"Thanks for the hospitality," Cole says.

"You are departing?"

"Going to see if I can round up my car. If it's all right with you, I'll park my skis by the door, pick em up in a while."

The pastor studies his book.

"You helped me out," Cole says. "Never got your name."

"Pastor will do," the Pastor says, not looking up.

"So thanks again. Pastor." Cole turns to leave.

"Gastation."

Cole turns back. "Sorry? I didn't get that."

The Pastor fixes his lenses on Cole. "Gas station. You'll need a tow, correct? Find John Ainsworth at the gas station. He will dispatch a tow truck."

"Good," Cole says. "I'll go find him."

"You won't get over the pass. No one will, for the duration." Behind the lenses, his eyes take Cole in, seemingly for the first time. "The best course is to go back down the mountain."

Cole nods, not in agreement. "Well, that's few a hundred miles out of my way. I'm kind of in a hurry. I'll find a shortcut."

The Pastor aims his lenses solemnly toward the ceiling.

"And I quote. *Never take no cut-offs. And hurry along as fast as you can.*"

Cole squints at him. "Say again?"

The Pastor's lenses level on Cole, blanking his eyes out.

"The best course is to go back down the mountain."

Chapter 3

The gas station Cole had passed coming into town has two pumps.
John Ainsworth is at one of them, coughing his lungs out while
fueling a big dirty truck. He is in his sixties, his overalls fit him
loosely. He watches the young stranger approach across the
shoveled concrete and already knows what his request will be.

"Hi," Cole says, halting nearby. "The Pastor said I should
talk to you about a tow."

Ainsworth's nozzle clicks off, he hangs the handle back in
the pump. "Well, go ahead."

Cole pauses, seeing the man isn't well.

"My car's down the road a ways. Up against a tree."

"Ray mentioned that one," Ainsworth says, tearing a
receipt out of the pump slot. "Couldn't hardly see it, buried as it
was." He hands the receipt into the window of the truck and begins
toward the office.

"Could you pull it out?" Cole asks, trailing him.

"Not physically, no."

Cole frowns. A high country wit. "I think I can probably
still drive it. It didn't hit that hard. I just need it hauled out."

"Roads ain't plowed. You try to drive it, you'll just end up
against another tree."

They enter the office, a cramped room with a wooden
counter that was in use well back into the last century. Ainsworth
takes command of a stool.

"Ray's been out on calls since four a.m.," he says. "You're
on in about two hours. You can set in the waiting room and read
ten-year old magazines, or just wander back later." He heaves into
another coughing fit, a wracking, hacking paroxysm that shakes his
shoulders and causes Cole to look elsewhere.

On the wall, an old framed print catches his eye – pioneers
with wagons and oxen, endeavoring to surmount deep mountain
snow. The freezing cold and their desperation feature prominently.

Ainsworth recovers himself and Cole ventures a question.

"Anyplace to eat around here?"

The older man regards him in wonder.

"Of course there's a place to eat. Did you think we were unfamiliar with the concept of a café?"

*

Cole has no problem finding the Cope Café. It is across the street. He slogs through the snow in the worn waterproof boots he always travels with and swings into the warmly lit eatery. It is steamy and smoky, redolent of bacon, with cracked floor tiles and abraded vinyl booths.

He takes a seat in one and has the curiosity of some well-seasoned locals along the counter. A stout woman in an apron pours him a cup of thick black coffee without asking.

"Thanks," Cole says. She wears a name tag, which he thinks quaint. "Althea, is it?"

"Is and always was. Decided what you want?"

"Didn't see a menu."

"Well that's all right, hon. We got a nice ham steak."

"Yes, please. With three eggs, over medium. I'm starving."

Althea regards him squarely. "Now that's a word I don't much care for."

He squints up at her.

"Starvation is a very grim affair. Folks get to eating leather. Harnesses and whatnot. Their shoes. Such is the drive for sustenance."

"Have you..?" Cole begins carefully.

"Of course not. I operate the Historical Society here in Cope. We feature artifacts and displays of times past. There was much hardship in these mountains."

Cole raises his brows, as if intrigued. "I'll have to stop by."

Althea moves for the kitchen. "We're open two to five."

The ham steak, when she brings it on a white plate, is high-quality meat, seared perfectly, and the eggs with bright orange yolks are from hens that forage loosely.

Cole nods his thanks. "Can I ask you something?"

"I suppose you could," Althea answers.

"Why does this town keep all the lights out at night?"

She stares down on him.

"So it looks like no one's at home."

Cole is left pondering her answer.

He returns to his plate, knife and fork in hand, and a man in a white Stetson and heavy jacket hoves into view. He wears official patches on his shoulders, a holstered handgun, plants himself before Cole's table.

"Good morning," he says, though for him it is clearly not.

"Morning."

"Deputy Ainsworth. You are..?"

Cole sees the name on the jacket. *Deputy Jim Ainsworth.*

"Cole Cantwell. Are you related to John Ainsworth?"

The deputy stares weightily at him, neglecting to answer.

"Just wondering," Cole says.

"What's your business here, Mr. Cantwell?"

For no good reason, threat is in the air. Cole feels irked.

"Uh…Well, I ran my car off the road coming up. It was kind of a white-out. So now I'm waiting for a tow truck to pull me out. So I can get briskly on my way."

The locals along the counter are rapt. Deputy Ainsworth scans Cole implacably.

"I thought I would get something to eat while I waited," Cole adds. "Which is why I'm sitting here. I just got my order. Ham and three eggs over medium."

It is evident Deputy Ainsworth lacks a sense of humor, yet Cole goes on.

"Althea, the waitperson, recommended the ham."

The air of threat is now permeated with an air of disbelief from the onlookers. The deputy's expression is walled.

"Let's see some identification."

"Sure. Did a law get broken?"

Deputy Ainsworth waits, not happily, while Cole seeks his wallet. He pulls his license out, the deputy scrutinizes it. He hands it back to him.

"Name matches the registration in the car."

"That's good, right? You've been inside my car?"

A dispatcher breaks in over the deputy's radio. He leans away, responding with a few terse words, turns back to Cole.

"Your car's been impounded. You have to pay a two-hundred-fifty-dollar fee to get it out. That computes daily."

"Computes daily," Cole says. "Why impound my car?"

The deputy considers him and Cole reads in his pouched and bloodshot eyes, his pale, nicked, clean-shaven face, a shuttered life, one close to the bottle.

"I impounded your car because you abandoned it on a public road." His radio squalls again and he leans in closer.

"Once you get that rice-burner in order, you might want to look for another destination. We're not really set up for tourism."

Cole watches Deputy Ainsworth stride out of the café. Along the counter, the locals are grinning.

Althea comes by, pours Cole more coffee.

"Althea?" he says.

"Yes?"

"Can you tell me where the impound lot is?"

"Across the street, hon. The gas station. Around the back." She leaves.

Cole considers his coffee cup, the blackness in it swirling.

Chapter 4

The impound lot constitutes a chain link fence surrounding a collection of seized automotive casualties – crapulent cars, stove-in accident victims, and there among the twisted steel and sheet metal is the Suburu, the windshield cracked, a dent in the nose.

Cole sighs, leaning against the fence as a rollback tow truck comes rattling into the alley behind him. He turns as it brakes to a stop. The driver jumps out – not what he expected. Close to his age, nice aspect, tough, girl-sized, wearing a canvas jacket, work boots. She looks over at Cole.

"Help you with something?"

Cole marvels at the obliqueness of the question. He gestures toward his imprisoned car.

"Are you responsible for this?"

"If it's in there, I towed it."

"Ah hah," he says. "Right. You must be Ray. John Ainsworth mentioned you."

"Rayann. John's daughter."

She approaches, sliding her sunglasses onto her head, examining Cole at closer range. Her eyes are steady and sharp, scored with faint lines. She is lean, well-formed, and he surmises she has led a rugged life. He grins unhappily.

"You guys are running quite a racket. I like the father-daughter angle. Between you two and Deputy Ainsworth… Wait. I bet you're related. The deputy's your uncle?"

Rayann pulls some folded paperwork from her pocket. "We call him J.A. Lots of folks related around here. What's your name?"

Cole introduces himself, she checks her list.

"Yeah. Got it. There's a fee to get your car out of jail."

"So I heard."

She throws her gaze on him. "Well? You want to pay it? I can process that inside and you can be on your way. Your car don't look that disabled and they're plowin the road down the mountain."

He nods, in a reasonable way, concealing a floodgate of wrath and anguish. "That all sounds nice. Only I'm a little short at the moment. Like two-hundred dollars short."

Rayann's eyes go over him, hazel in color, he decides. "You don't have some kind of card?"

"No," Cole says, "I do have a card. But if you ran it, we'd just have to start all over."

"Shoot it down, would they?"

"It would crash like a plane."

That leaves them silent.

"Well, Cole," Rayann says, "You're pretty well fucked."

He is quick to agree. "Fucked good, Rayann. Any other possibilities occur to you?"

She considers the question, looking off, her fine brows set.

"You could come back tonight with a pair of boltcutters and snap that lock. Of course, if J.A., who's on the job night and day, runs into you, he'll book you into County down there. Somewhat of a hellhole, what I've heard."

Cole senses a challenge, rises to it. "Where would I find boltcutters?"

Rayann doesn't back down. "My dad has tools. Doesn't necessarily keep track of em all."

He takes her in, with admiration.

"We gotta have a drink sometime."

She meets his intentions directly. "If you're still loose tomorrow, look me up."

And then she is off on other business, Cole watching her stride to the tow truck. She steps up on the running board, slides into the cab gracefully, slams the door. The truck steams past.

He likes that. How she goes on her way. How she never even glances at him. Not once.

*

Light leaves Cope early, the snowbound buildings dropping into blue shadow as the surrounding peaks close off the day. By that hour, Cole has engineered the acquisition of John Ainsworth's boltcutters, secured from a cluttered bench in the garage. Ainsworth is out at the pumps, coughing up a storm while fueling a motorhome.

The basement in the church is not welcoming. The Pastor, at his desk when Cole walks by, never looks up, says nothing. Cole passes the time on the cot below, charging his phone, drowsing. When he goes out the front door with his skis and his backpack, the church is dark and cold and he is happy to leave it forever behind.

The hamlet is as murky, frigid dwellings heaped with snow, icicles bared like fangs. The last few lights, over a doorway, behind a curtain, blink out, and he feels very alone.

As he treads the brittle walkways, a sound carries to him, and it causes him to stop, train his ears.

It is a howling. Distant. Claiming the twilight. Two or three sets of throat cords pitched into a feral, fevered cry.

The howling dies off.

Cole stands in the stark shadows, staring toward the white crags that loom over Cope.

Then he is moving again, his boots punching ice, the frost of his breath hanging. It isn't good tidings, that cry from the mountain reaches, it doesn't forecast safety, a clear road.

He heads down the alley behind the gas station. His penlight pins a beam ahead, lights a dumpster. He raises the lid, probing flattened cardboard, finding the boltcutters he has concealed there.

The wash of headlights sweep the alley. Tires crunch over cold ground. Cole cuts his penlight, flattens into the shadows.

A white 4X4 with sheriff's insignia cruises past the end of the alley. He gets a profile of Deputy Ainsworth, features dim.

When the sound of the truck diminishes, Cole leaves the dumpster, continuing down the alley, blending into the night.

*

Later, Cole slouches on the cot, the furnace throbbing. His phone is fully charged and he gazes into the light of the screen, unhappy with what it is telling him.

No Service

He has difficulty finding sleep, thinking of Sandra, but when he does sleep, he sleeps hard, not awakening until mid-day.

The sun is out. Trudging along banked snow, he passes an old bungalow and is informed by a placard that it serves as the Cope Historical Society Museum.

He decides to have a look.

Approaching the porch, a bearded face watches him from the panes of a window.

The front door is unlocked.

Pale light crosses a mannequin adorned with a floppy hat. Its beard is painfully phony, the figure simulating a forbear, a pioneer, and inciting in Cole little desire to press on.

The museum is poorly lit, dusty, musty, cluttered with the unremarkable. He passes a blacksmith's anvil, farming implements, a glass case featuring a collection of straight-razors.

Ahead is another room.

Three dummies slump around a campfire of rocks. By their period garments, they are emigrants, father, mother, child, a blackened cooking pot between them. Cole peers down at the child's metal dinner plate. It holds only dry twigs and tiny bones.

He looks to the wall exhibit nearby.

The Donner Party in the Sierra Nevada
The group of 87 left Springfield, Illinois with their wagons and headed west... The Hastings Cut-Off Proves No Shortcut... Snowbound in the worst winter of the Sierra Nevada... Five Month Ordeal... consuming mice, hides and string before being driven to cannibalism... Rescue Party Finds Gruesome Scene ... hair, bones, skulls and half-eaten limbs... Jacob Donner was discovered with his arms and legs cut off and his heart and liver removed...
"Remember, never take no cutoffs and hurry along as fast as you can."
Virginia Reed, Donner Party survivor

Scanning the 19th century photographs, Cole takes in the hardscrabble misery, the bleak, raw features. The tormented gazes, the unforgiving iron stares.

"You found us."

Althea has appeared behind him.

He looks to her, unsettled

"So, how many of them made it?"

"About half. Females survived the males two-to-one. The men tended to lose their minds. It was the women who held things together."

Cole senses some bias on her part.

"Interesting."

"Yes."

"This cannibalism thing," he begins. "I mean, the families… They didn't…"

She grasps his question.

"They separated the kin. You don't eat your own."

Act of decency or practical measure, Cole envisions the raw horror of it. "No," he agrees. "That wouldn't be right."

It is time to leave. Althea's firm gaze, the unspeakable that has been spoken, leaves him uneasy. It takes him the rest of the day to shake the visit, and a few beers with someone companionable.

Chapter 5

That evening the Cope Café undergoes its nightly transition, becoming lively with country music and mountain folk – the wild, the lonely, the snowbound. As the Pastor is reluctant to loan out the church, the cafe is the only other sheltered venue that accommodates loud, drunken gatherings.

Cole has contacted Rayann and she agrees to meet him there. They come in early and secure a booth at the rear. They order beers and that leads to an order of boilermakers. Maybe he offers her a break from the norm, something different, because she seems to welcome his company. He certainly welcomes hers. As more customers pour in, the volume level rises to an uproar. They speak loudly to be heard, chase shots of cheap whiskey with cold lager, and their conversation grows spirited.

Cole brings up his afternoon. "So I had a creepy time in Cope today."

"You went to the museum."

He squints at her.

"It's a small town," she says. "Not even that."

They hoist the beers, the shots.

"Next subject," he says. "Did you happen to mention anything about boltcutters to J.A.?"

"Didn't have to. He already knows you're a pistol."

"A pistol..? You mean like, I'm half-cocked?"

She declines to pursue that.

"He cruise by the impound lot?"

"He did."

"He has little else to do."

Cole likes resting his eyes on her. "Glad you could make it. I need the company about now."

"I'll sit with you a while. Unless you start makin a fool of yourself."

"I'm hoping that's behind me."

She smiles.

He says, "I heard something kind of odd last night."
Rayann watches him, waiting.
"Howling. Like wolves. Up on the slopes."
"Yeah?"
"Yeah. But there are no wolves in the Sierra Nevada range. Are there even wolves in California?"
Her eyes hold more than she's saying. "What's that leave?"
"I don't know. A party? Some locals getting high? A weird snow ritual, maybe?"
She grins. He is entertaining her, with his wit, or his naivete, he knows not.
"What if I told you it was The Old Man of the Mountain?"
"I'd say, what fun zone are we in now?"
The country music bangs and pulses, a dancing couple trip past their table, bootheels dragging the floor. She watches them lurch away.
"Local legend. Some crazy settler is said to live up there. Supposed to be a hundred years old."
"That's kind of scary."
"You don't believe it at all."
"Well. It's colorful, I'll say that for it."
A waitress goes by, Cole signals her. He's left with his empty glass upraised.
"That didn't work," she says.
"Not remotely."
"I enjoy the way you talk."
"You do?" He is glad to hear it, warmed by whiskey and ready to take on the night ahead.
"You sound like a character," she says.
"Good or bad?"
Rayann assesses him. "Both, probably."
They let that rest.
"So," he says. "Do cell phones work here?"
"Hardly. It's landlines up this way. Tryin to make a call?"
"Don't know why. No one's waiting to pounce on it."
She reads him. "You got a girl-problem? Try the phone in

the gas station office."

His admiration of her expands. The waitress returns.

"Another round?"

Cole looks to Rayann. She says, "Hit us, Lonnie."

Lonnie is off again.

"So how long have you lived here?" Cole asks.

"Longer than I ought to."

"Why don't you leave?"

"Thought long and hard about it. I grew up here. My family goes way back. Where's a mountain gal like me gonna go? And I have a boy. Don't want to be haulin him all over, looking to fit in somewhere I don't belong."

"How old's your boy?"

"Ty will be eleven."

"You don't look old enough," he says. He means it as a compliment, but it doesn't quite come off. He sees her bristle and the waitress Lonnie leans in between them, delivers their beers and shots, is gone instantly.

"That's the way it is around here," Rayann says. "You get hooked up too early. And get unhooked too late."

Cole is left on uncertain ground. "So are you hooked or unhooked?"

She slams the shot, chases it with beer. "If I was hooked, I wouldn't be sittin here with some stranger passin through."

He administers his own sequence. "I'm not all that strange."

"And you'd be in trouble. You'd be dead, or they'd have to airlift you to the nearest trauma center."

"Between you and me, Rayann, I've already been to the trauma center. Now I'm having a drink with a mountain gal who lives in awe of her great big jealous ex-boyfriend."

"Ex-husband."

"If I'm crowding you, just let me know."

"Count on it."

"I have been. Then I ran out of fingers."

That engages her. She laughs. He is pleased. The café

booms around them and her thoughts turn inward.

"I used to live in awe of him," she says. "Now I live in fear of him. So does everyone else. Wade Deal wasn't always a monster, but that's the only word for him now. My boy's the only good part of that mistake." She raises her eyes to Cole. "Fear. Fear and blood. That's all that's holdin this place together."

"Whoa," Cole says.

Rayann opens her handbag. "And you just wanted a casual conversation."

"Like you said, I'm a stranger passing through."

She puts twenty dollars on the table. "I know you're pressed, so let me buy this one. You got somewhere to stay tonight?"

He regrets his haste. He feels unchivalrous. "I'm not out in the cold. Listen…"

She silences him with a gesture, seeing glances aimed their way. She speaks quietly and he strains to hear her words. "J.A.'s down in Topaz havin dinner with his ex-wife. If you found those cutters, you got two hours to get off the mountain before he passes you comin up."

She stands from the booth. Their night had started off well, but it isn't ending that way. He blames himself. He's always trying to work an angle, and this girl is a fox, genuine, natural. She confirms it when all he can come up with is thanking her.

"Like to see one of us make it out of here," she says, and then she weaves through the crowd and is out the door, and he remains there, a couple sliding in across from him, yammering to each other as they grab her seat.

Cole is justly abandoned and he's sorry to see her go.

*

The rest of the night goes no better. On his solitary course, stealing through the darkness of the alley with his gear, he raises the lid of the dumpster and aims his penlight inside. After scattering a lot of trash he comes to the realization that the boltcutters he concealed there are gone. Desperation edges in, he strides along the chain link imprisoning his car.

The Suburu is entombed under a layer of snow. He feels called on to do something.

Cole scales the chain link, dragging up with him an old piece of carpet freed from the dumpster. He throws it over the barbed wire at the top of the fence and boosts himself over. He clambers down the other side of the fence, jumps free, pushes snow off the Suburu's windshield, slides in behind the wheel. He keeps an emergency key in a magnetic tin under the dashboard.

From his seat, he sizes up the padlock chaining the double gates closed, decides one good bang should do it. He fits the key in the ignition, turns it. Nothing.

Dead battery.

He slams the steering wheel.

Back in the basement, furnace light wavering, Cole sits on the cot, jacket zipped tight, his phone held near. The screen is black, a recognizable symbol visible.

Dead battery.

Chapter 6

Night passes slowly, sleep intermittent, his thoughts flaring. With the amber of morning, a dream evolves. He's been moving through a passage with his father and they step out onto a ledge. Far below, a river thunders. He watches a rickety craft being rushed downstream.

"What's that?" Cole asks.

Jack Cantwell identifies it. "That's you."

When Cole drags his way from the basement he has no real plan for the day. He has the use of the church bathroom, goes through his routine and heads down the hallway. The Pastor catches up with him at the front door. Cole attempts a greeting, but the man seems unacquainted with pleasantries.

"I'm going to be requiring rent."

Cole regards him, pained.

"I'm a little short at the moment, Pastor."

The Pastor's lenses remain trained on him.

"As are we all. How much do you have in your wallet?"

"It's pretty lonely in there."

The Pastor waits. Cole drags his wallet out. They peer in.

"The church will take half."

Bravely, Cole hands him a twenty.

*

When Cole walks into the gas station office, John Ainsworth is propped against the counter, involved in a coughing fit, Rayann holds the desk, trying to organize a chaos of statements and orders, the landline is jangling and a pickup is honking out at the pumps.

"You're going home today, dad," Rayann says.

"Am not."

"Yes, you are."

A sturdy boy appears in the entrance doorway. He has a short bristly haircut, hoists a daypack, and ignoring the cold, wears shorts, a T shirt and laced boots. Rayann glowers.

"Why aren't you on the bus?"

"It didn't come," the boy says.

"You are not missin another day of school, Ty."

Ainsworth hacks. "I'll run him down there,"

Rayann seizes the phone. "No you won't – *Ainsworth's*," she yells into the receiver.

John Ainsworth flags the boy. "Let's go, Ty-boy."

"*Dad...*" Rayann warns, then to the caller, "*Well what's the holdup? Been waitin weeks on this.*"

The horn stabs out from the pickup at the pumps.

Rayann, frayed, glances that way.

"I'll get it," Cole says, heading outside.

The late-model pickup stands out because of its hulking size and its color, some variation of sunburst-orange. In the cab, two middle-aged hunters in high-end camouflage parkas wait impatiently for Cole to serve them.

He crosses the concrete, arrives at the driver's door. The man looks down on him through polarized eyewear.

"Real fast-paced around here."

Cole is intent on staying even and being useful. "What can I do for you?" he asks.

"What can you do for me? How about fueling my rig?" The driver hands down a credit card. "The diesel."

Restraining an anti-social response, Cole slots the card and unhooks the pump handle. The gas filler lid pops open on the flank of the truck. Cole drives the nozzle in and returns the card.

"And get the windshield," the driver orders.

Cole locks the pump open, picks up the bucket and squeegee. It takes a stool to reach the windshield and he kicks it into place. While he scrapes the glass clean, the two hunters hold a running commentary on the backwoods environment they find themselves in.

"Hicks in the sticks."

"Fucking Cope. What do they do here?"

"They fuck. They watch television."

"Sounds about right."

"You bring that scent-blocker?"

"Between that and the camo, we're invisible."

"Trophy buck, here we come."

"No less than a twelve-pointer."

Cole finishes the glass and jumps down to squeeze the pump handle off. As he hands the receipt up, he notices a rifle racked across the rear cab window. It is an expensive piece, glossy walnut and blue steel, precision German telescopic scope.

The driver leers down at him.

"That's my thunderstick. And no, you can't touch it."

His partner brays, the driver takes his leave.

Cole watches the truck glide away. Rayann walks up and joins him. "There's no deer in the alpine now," she says. "They're all downslope where the forage is."

"Then they'll have a bad day."

"That they will. You want a job?"

He studies her.

"Temporary?" she says. "I got a lot of big rounds at home need to be turned into cordwood. You ever work a splitter?"

He hasn't. He isn't even sure what a splitter is.

"Log splitter," she says.

"Oh, yeah."

"You have?"

"Some."

Rayann regards him dubiously. "Well, then. Between that and the pumps you could pick up enough hourly to drive home in high style."

"I could get ahold of that. What're you paying?"

"Honest wages," she says, walking back to the office.

She is all business today, and she doesn't dress up, but the woman she embodies isn't disguised by work clothes. One thing more for Cole to admire.

*

John Ainsworth's house is a hundred-year-old bungalow the harsh climate has stripped to the siding. A covered porch with tapered columns spans the front width, a pair of hollow-eyed dormers break the roofline. From a chimney of fractured river stone, woodsmoke lofts into the dense white sky.

Cole Cantwell is in the side yard working the log splitter, a battered hydraulic unit he doesn't know how to operate on first encounter. Watching the boy wedge rounds apart, he learns quickly. Now Cole is slamming large shaggy trunk pieces onto the log cradle, working the control arm, valving the splitting head down, feeling accomplished as the steel presses into the grain of the fir and cracks the round apart.

The splitter pressures twenty tons, its little gas motor chugging, drifting oily fumes. Ty proves unafraid of hard labor, wheelbarrowing heavy loads away and stacking the split wood neatly under a long shed roof. The kid is hardy, strong-willed, and not altogether impressed with Cole's prowess as a woodsman. They voice a conversation over the hammering of the motor.

"So how much work we got here?" Cole asks.

Ty dumps a wheelbarrow load. "Bout eight cords."

Cole watches him build the pile of cordwood.

"How much work is that?"

The boy turns. By his expression, he holds the question as simple-minded.

"A cord's four-by-four-by-eight. And we got times eight."

Cole eyes him. "So if I understand your math, we'll be at it for a while." He rocks a round onto the log cradle.

"We burn wood all year," Ty says, bringing the wheelbarrow up. Cole crushes the wedge down into the wood. It rents apart with a loud crack.

"Old John," the boy says, "he used to put in ten cords by himself every season. Before he got all sick."

His eyes are on Cole, taking him in, measuring him, no longer the eyes of a child. It trips an uneasy note in Cole, an interloper from the lowlands.

"Old John. That's what you call your grandad?"

Ty pitches wood into the wheelbarrow. It shudders, clanks. "He don't call me grandson. He calls me Ty-boy. So I call him Old

John. I call my dad Wade."

He wheels off nonchalantly, but the flash of turmoil that crosses his face betrays him. Cole considers ways he can bridge the subject.

"How long's your dad been gone?"

The boy upheaves the wheelbarrow at the woodpile. "Five or six years. He ain't dead, you know." He throws Cole a defiant look. "You comin to my birthday party?"

Cole squints at him. "When is it?"

"Tomorrow. Mom's takin me to Macchus and Ida's. That's my dad's folks."

Cole is not a great mixer. Far be it from him to gather with strangers he has nothing in common with. More distant is attending a strange child's birthday party.

"I gotta be somewhere," he tells the boy. He takes in the multitude of fir rounds. "Here."

"Oh," Ty says, and bends to his work.

The kid sounds disappointed, and that surprises Cole. They hardly know each other.

"Your dad's coming, isn't he?"

"He never comes. Not Christmas neither. He says parties and presents makes you weak."

Cole is learning more about the menacing Wade Deal than he cares to. "You don't agree?"

"Hell no. I like gifts. You don't have to bring me one."

Ty fits cordwood in place, the stacks growing, and Cole reaches an understanding. The boy is starved for a healthy male adult, a guardian, a companion. Though he knows himself to be unreliable, it leaps from his mouth, a statement he is certain he will regret even as it is spoken.

"All right," he says. "I'm in."

A kind of light comes into the boy's face. "Really?"

"Beats the splitter." Another rash comment, steering himself further into unmapped terrain.

The boy happily arranges wood. "You like my mom?"

It is a straight question and rates a straight answer. Cole

likes his mom a lot, but that response is just going to put him further into jeopardy. "Well, sure," he says. "Nice lady. She gave me work."

The boy is waiting for more. "And she'll talk to me," Cole adds. "Usually. Not many in Cope willing to have a conversation."

The boy's face clouds over.

"They're scared," he says

Cole's uneasiness sharpens. "Scared of what?"

Beyond the boy, Cole notices John Ainsworth observing them from the shadows of the porch. Doing something he shouldn't. He draws a cigarette from his lip, eyes slatted.

The boy says, "You live here in Cope, you don't run your mouth. And you don't call outsiders in."

His eyes go over Cole again, eyes ages older than he.

Cole says, "That like a town ordinance or something?"

Beyond, John Ainsworth drops his butt in a tin can on the rail, goes back inside the house.

Cole sees the smoke from the chimney shift on the wind. The sky has no reach, packed in, closed.

"Looks like snow," he says.

The boy studies him, silent.

*

By lantern light, Cole's naked shadow is printed across one wall of the basement. He's rigged a shower – a galvanized washtub, a bucket of water heated on the sheet metal of the furnace. He has waited for the bucket to steam, uses a towel to grab the bail, gratefully tips the hot water over his soaped-up hair, his shoulders.

Rivulets drip off him, musical against the tin of the tub. He glances toward his shadow and his shadow follows suit, glancing toward some nonexistent point.

Shadows, he reflects, can see no farther than the thrower of the shadow, and offer no foresight.

Powder banks itself against the narrow window.

Tomorrow weighs on him.

Chapter 7

"You're a game one," Rayann says to Cole that morning, "Comin along on this outing." She drives, he is in the passenger seat. Her Jeep is drafty, rides hard and bangs loudly over uneven asphalt, the present asphalt no more than a damp gully between drifts piled shoulder-high. Daylight stitches itself through the evergreens branched above.

"I made a deal," Cole says.

She is giving him the once-over, her frank inspection picking up a wealth of compromising data. Cole, as groomed and presentable as he's going to get on this mountain, feels stripped of cover, foolhardy. He turns to the boy. "Right, Ty?"

Ty wears a watchcap down over his ears, a bulky coat.

"If it ain't a good fit, you can wait in the Jeep."

Cole grins. The little fucker.

"They're in-laws," Rayann says, keeping the Jeep on course over the slick surface. "But they're still family. I start cutting relations loose, it's gonna get real lonely in Cope."

The boy is gaming on his mobile in the back seat. The device keeps honking, which is getting on Cole's skinned nerves.

"Well," he says, "like Ty pointed out, I have plan B."

"We keep a sleeping bag in the back there," Rayann tells him. "Case it gets frosty."

"You are far too good to me."

She beams. "I'm bettin you're gonna ace this one. You clean up decent and you're tolerable company. Macchus and Ida aren't gonna eat you."

Cole shoots a look. "Funny you should phrase it that way."

Rayann utters a husky laugh. "Relax, Cole."

Shortly, the Jeep slows for a driveway cut out of the drifts. As they turn into it, Cole stares out at a welded sculpture serving as a mailbox. The "DEALS" a sign announces, atop what seems to be a laughing bear, the mail slot its mouth. For Cole, it only emphasizes how removed he is from whimsey.

The driveway is lengthy, cutting through the snowy trees. It ends at clearing where stands a neat modular house, a steel barn, a yellow backhoe, and a motorhome under a custom shelter.

Rayann parks before the modular and the three of them emerge from the Jeep. Cole takes in the surroundings. Someone has been busy with a snow-blower, the property obsessively well-kept.

A woman comes out the front door. She has a gray ponytail and is dressed warmly, her pants tucked into shearling boots. She issues a bright smile, motioning her guests in.

"That's Ida," Rayann says.

The guests troop forward. Rayann and Ida exchanged a brief hug. The grandmother exclaims over the boy.

"Gettin mighty big, Ty."

"Can't help it."

"I made you a special cake, Birthday Boy. Go in and shake hands with Grandpa Macchus like the little man you are."

All of this without once looking at Cole. He perceives it will be one of those occasions, a forced and frigid two or three hours of stilted exchanges amid the agonizing inching of the clock. As they enter the living area his expectations are reinforced by the appearance of Macchus Deal, large as a ledge, his great slab of hand extended, a face of granite.

Ty marches up to him, dwarfed. "Shake, Macchus."

Macchus does so, engulfing the boy's hand. "Well. Grip like a pair of channel locks." He effected a lipless grin, rows of teeth splitting the rock of his face. "We got some birthday doins today."

The boy scrambles past him, racing for the kitchen. Grandma Ida swiftly follows.

Rayann reaches out and touches the huge man's sleeve, and Cole finds that interesting, that there is no embrace.

"Good to see you, dad."

"And lookin more beautiful every day," Macchus says. "You hungry? Ida's cookin up... something or other..."

He is distracted, Cole becoming the center of his attention.

Something foreign has crossed his threshold.

Rayann offers him up.

"This is Cole, dad. Cole, meet Macchus."

Cole steps in to shake hands. "Cole Cantwell."

Macchus Deal's grin is no more. His rocky knuckles brush Cole's hand.

"Cole," he rumbles. "What brings you this way?" His eyes, bleached by time, search out answers.

Cole presents himself in simple terms. "I got caught in a blizzard coming over the pass. My car was towed to the gas station. That's where I met Rayann." He looks to her for confirmation.

Rayann nods brightly.

Macchus considers each of them, as if trying to assimilate the true meaning of all this.

"Cole's doin some work around the place," Rayann explains. "Ty really wanted him to come to the party. Here he is."

Her stepfather's brooding features dash the light of her grin. "He's not intendin to stay on, is he?"

Cole and Rayann look at one another.

"Nope," they both say.

Macchus evidences some relief. "You wouldn't find much to occupy yourself, Cole. It's a well-ordered system, Cope. Think of it as a tightly knit cooperative. Each member serves a function that benefits the whole. You'd be su-per-fulless."

He waits for this wisdom to sink in.

"Right," Cole says. "I get that."

His host's teeth show again, yellow as old bone. He says, "Rayann, why not see if Ida needs any help."

"Glad to," Rayann says, and glad she is, whisking off.

Cole marks her absence with regret. He and the grandfather find themselves before the hearth. It is, Cole notices, lit by gas jets and constructed of simulated stones. He thinks that disillusioning. Scattered across the mantel are framed photos. He glances over them while warming himself at what passes for authenticity.

"Puts out pretty good heat," he says.

"Propane," Macchus points out. "We have holding tanks for everything. Oil, gasoline. Septic. The well pumps from a thousand-year aquifer. Generators. We are self-sufficient here. Storeroom's stocked with bulk goods. Commercial freezer…"

He looks down on Cole from the crags of his face.

"If the world ended today, we would live on."

"Must be good to know that," Cole says.

He is reluctant to delve further, but delving further is ordained, a part forced on him in his capacity as an intruder. "You got all your firepower in place?"

Macchus inspects him for ridicule.

"We have an armory. Do you have a survival plan?"

"Uh, no." Cole stares into the gas flames. "No, I really don't. I figure I'll just wing it."

Macchus shifts his stance, like a wall settling.

"You don't believe society is about to blow itself to hell?"

"Always," Cole says. "Societies come and go."

Macchus rests a boot on the flat of the hearth, outsized, square, leather unmarked. "When this present society goes, and provender is scarce, the sky black, and the depraved, the hordes from hell, appear on your street, you'll wish you did have a plan."

Cole is impressed with his imagination. He can see it himself, day like night, a ragged snarl of raw meat eaters fanning out through the suburbs. "Maybe," he agrees. "But given that picture, why would I *want* to survive?"

Macchus drops his shaggy brows.

"Order. God and order. That's what keeps us from becoming animals. In terrible times, do not surrender. Stand your ground."

The notion strikes Cole as inspirational.

"Find your center," he says.

Macchus ponders that.

"Yes."

Ida approaches them, hands her husband a hot mug. Hands a second mug to Cole without a word, without eye contact.

"Thank you," Cole says as she leaves them.

Macchus swills hot buttered rum, steam curling.

"What is it you do, Cole?"

That dreaded question. When asked, he no longer launches into a shining summary of his exploits, because after all the effort it still sounded like he lived in his car. His bio was now abbreviated.

"This and that," he says. "Travel. Do some skiing. Downhill. Some backcountry."

Macchus surveys him. Cole has the sensation he is conversing with an outcropping.

"I wonder if you've ever seen the real backcountry?"

Cole is snared, has no choice but to continue. "I don't know. Seemed pretty real when I did a face-plant and ended up with a mouthful of it."

Sadly, Macchus sways his great head.

"Young men and their follies."

"Right," Cole says. "I guess you've been there." He recalls he's holding a mug of hot rum, drinks from it.

Macchus says, "I have a son who's tested me sorely."

Cole hesitates. They are tipping into another hazardous area. "That would be Wade?"

Macchus looks on him grimly. The fissures of his face are deep, like erosion channeled into basalt. How old is this man, Cole wonders. How many years does it take to earn a visage like that?

"I taught him to live right and to live hard," Macchus says. "He rejected the clubs, the activities, the comforts. He peeled the apple down to its core. But Wade is headstrong and has a hard time abiding by rules."

Disquieted, Cole has broken eye-contact. Macchus is terrible to look on, like some wrathful giant from a biblical excavation. Cole instead scans the aged photos on the mantel, hardy, well-worn folk, four or five generations of tenacious pioneer stock fastened to the land like taproots.

"Rules," Macchus says. "Upholding tradition. The Deals have always honored their past. Our forbears survived the winter of forty-seven at the Donner Lake encampment."

Cole racks his mind for a response.

"You get through that, you can get through about anything."

The elder's focus has joined Cole's, they behold the framed ancestors, the Deal's of the past.

"We respect their will. They did what had to be done."

The sepia-toned dead stare out at Cole, an historic gallery of carbon ghosts, cellulose apparitions.

"The will to prevail," Macchus says. "It's in the blood."

Chapter 8

The birthday party proceeds. They assemble around the boy who is tearing gift wrap from an oblong case. His face flushes with astonishment, he already knows what this will be. He frees the last of the paper, unsnaps the hard plastic case, frees his substantial present, something he's dreamed of.

"Wow! A compound bow! And hunting arrows!"

Proudly, he brandishes the bow, a complex contraption rigged with pulleys and cables, a quiver of feathered shafts attached.

"My gosh, Ty," Ida exclaims. "That's beautiful."

Ty removes a broadhead arrow, enamored with the bladed tip. Rayann's expression is one of foreboding. Her eyes flick over to Cole, his own expression acknowledges her misgivings – mayhem awaits. The boy's grandfather helpfully outlines the bow's features.

"This is the junior model. Forty pounds draw weight. You could pin a racoon to a tree with that."

Ty's imagination soars. "So cool! Thank you! Thank you!"

"We're bowhunters all the way back, son."

Ida stands. "Well, I'd better get supper on." She waves at Ty. "Then we'll have that cake with eleven candles on it."

She goes into the kitchen, Ty fondles his bow, occupied with stalking fantasies, Macchus warmly overseeing him.

"I brought him something, too," Cole confides to Rayann. She is still trying to come to grips with the boy's gift and narrows her eyes suspiciously. "What?"

"Uh." Cole begins. "It's a T-shirt. From the Sierra Club? I found it in my backpack."

Rayann's eyes close completely.

Cole seeks to improve his position. "It's never been worn."

Rayann's eyes open on him. "That's not goin over."

"Left it the car," Cole says.

"Better go get it."

*

Cole leans into the Jeep to retrieve the boy's present, which he knows is paltry but is better than nothing. He hopes it will at least hold off dark looks for stiffing the child by attending his birthday with no presents at all.

Walking back to the house, a light snags his attention. It spills out of the doorway of a small outbuilding behind the modular house. Ida's upraised voice comes to him.

"Darn it."

Approaching the doorway, Cole sights into a white room with a large white freezer, white tile, a white sink, and in a white apron, Ida, in profile. She's at a butcher block holding her hand out, and the beads of blood dripping from her index finger gleam crimson against the sanitary brightness.

While Cole looks on, Ida winds a white cloth around her finger, then resumes her work. Now a joint of meat is visible on the block and in her other a hand, a bone saw.

She begins cutting through the joint, a small woman, but strong, skilled. Trained.

The saw rasps through flesh, bone, gristle.

When Cole comes back inside the house, Rayann looks him over and makes comment. "Kind of skittish, aren't you? Something happen out there?"

"Huh?" Cole says, a little ashen. "I'm fine."

The gift, the T-shirt, is bestowed and the boy avoids Cole for the rest of the evening. At the dinner table, set with Ida's heirloom china, all are seated. She brings a platter in, ruddy meat in a dark sauce, and Macchus does the honors, slicing portions, loading plates. He uses a bone-handled carver, is deft with it.

"Thought we were runnin low, Ida. But once again you have proven me wrong."

"Just part of my job," Ida jokes, and Cole notes the bandage now neatly taped on her wounded forefinger.

She places servings in front of each guest to exclamations of approval, less Cole, who sits regarding his portion as though it might suddenly pulsate.

"Oh boy," Ty says, eyes big. "You made this, Grandma?"

"Looks and smells wonderful, Ida," Rayann says. Her attention is on Cole, monitoring him, waiting for his next hapless maneuver, and he doesn't let her down.

"What exactly is this?" he inquires politely. "If I can ask?"

The question clamps Ida's mouth. She stabs a bite of meat with her fork and Macchus comes to her aid.

"It's as good as any restaurant," he intones.

Rayann digs into her plate. "Delicious."

"I'll say," the boy chirps.

Macchus chuckles. "Voice slidin around. He's at that age."

Ida has something to clarify.

"Well," she begins. "You just make do with what you are provided, is all. Our people take a situation and make it work. My goodness, that's why they call this place Cope."

Agreement is murmured. Cole, fork and knife in hand, steels himself, working up to placing a small square of dinner in his mouth, chewing it.

"Try some of my yams with that," Ida says.

She locks eyes with him, eyes of flint, recognizing him that evening for the first and last time.

*

The Jeep's headlights cut into the darkness as they drive down the icy road toward home. The boy has fallen asleep in the back, Cole sits in the passenger seat, meditating on this juncture of his life. Rayann has the wheel, entertaining her own restless thoughts.

"So you goin weird on me?" she asks Cole.

Cole turns his head toward her. "You ask me that after bringing me up here?"

"Brought yourself, as I remember."

"Uh huh."

"You didn't eat," she says.

"Guess I'm off my feed."

Rayann exhales. "Jesus, Cole. It was just lamb."

He receives that darkly. They drive in silence for a while.

"You have an interesting talk with Macchus?" she asks.

"Oh sure," he says.

"What about?"

"Well, let's see. We talked a little about the Donner Party. We talked about the end times, the hordes of hell appearing on our streets. Oh, and Wade. How he peeled the apple down to its core. All-in-all, it was a pretty good round-table of existential concerns."

Rayann stares ahead, headlights gliding across pale trees.

"Damn," she finally says. "If you aren't a wonder."

Chapter 9

On a forest service road in the alpine, the knobby tires of the hulking sunburst-orange pickup churn through virgin snow. The driver's name is Boardman and he is keen, almost desperate, to engage the hunt, as is his passenger, Rayford. They talk in a desultory manner, pines sliding past, each man fully outfitted – pricey camo parkas, finely wrought rifles, 300 magnum ammo. Advanced optics. Cold weather boots. Big game knives, sharper than sharp.

The pickup, Boardman's pride, is an example of rolling brute force, its lines carved out of steel. Blunt front end, giant treads, lofty ground clearance. The occupants ride high and go anywhere. Seventy grand, fully optioned. The 7.3 turbo-diesel wafted the two of them up from the heat of the valley and now they are riding through the snowy crispness of God's country searching out afternoon sport.

The pair gets along pretty well, Boardman thrice divorced and Rayford walked out on regularly. Ex-wives held that they were the only two who could stand each other's company, and that is true for the most part, disagreements are few, and a flask of Kentucky bourbon has a way of ironing out uneven ground and gilding the day with a warm animation. As things move now, a copper glow attends their progress into the wilds.

The flask Boardman takes a swallow from is leather-bound. His eyes on the route ahead, he hands it over to Rayford.

"The nose is round," Boardman says. "With notes of caramel and fucking peat smoke."

Rayford swills some. "Tastes like a fresh coat of varnish."

"Good in the morning, right? Last ex claimed I was an alcoholic."

The other man studies the flask. "You got your initials stamped here. That might be something."

Boardman scowls. "They always get the kids on the custody. I have a couple twenty-somethings out there, wouldn't know em if I ran em over."

"When it's done," Rayford says, "don't waste time. Grab hold of someone else." He hands the flask back.

"If you fall off the horse…" Boardman has another taste.

Rayford stares into a past confrontation. "Just do what I say. Is that asking too much? You can go out and shop all goddamn day."

"My problem with wives," Boardman says, "they keep turning into the same woman."

"They repeat themselves."

"One bonus being single, I don't have to pick up after myself."

"And you don't. A pigsty"

"I'm happy."

"What's that?" Rayford asks, his eyes on something ahead.

Boardman brakes. The windshield frames the snowy road, a line of dark tracks punched across it.

"My friend," he smiles, "the game is on."

They exchange a hand slap.

*

Boardman and Rayford open the truck bed and sort out gear. The aluminum-frame snowshoes come in handy. Fitted in place, the two hoist backpacks, sling their rifles and they are off.

They quickly pick up a trail, the snow deepening, the tracks they are following now leg holes rather than the stamp of cloven hooves. They move quietly, so they think, their breath streaming, exhaled with their exertions, and the forest takes them, gathers them in its boughs. They fade into the white gloom.

After a while, all signs of their quarry vanish, then the trail itself vanishes, the snowy earth cleaving toward a ridge, and they have nothing to follow at all. They climb to the ridge, which lines a draw the snow has piled into. Across the draw it is heavily wooded.

Both men are huffing.

"Don't know if we're gonna reclaim this," Rayford says.

"We'll surprise something," Boardman says.

"Dead shots here."

"Guaranteed by the maker."

"Three group inside an inch, hundred yards or less."

Their progress brings them to a downed cedar blocking their path and the flush of the liquor has long dissipated and they are tired, the snowshoes are hard work and neither is interested in pushing on. In unspoken accord, they quit there, surveying the stillness, the gray of the skies, the gunmetal terrain. A gust stirs powder off the ridge, they watch it uncoil like vapor, and it is here that the call, the bleat, comes to them.

They unsling their rifles. Kneeling, Rayford trains his scope into the thick of the trees across the draw. Light snow falls. Intent, Boardman looks on.

The call comes again, a soft grunting.

They glance at each other in triumph.

"Buck," Boardman mouths. "Big one."

Rayford, steely, nods. His eyes are still on his partner when a streak splits the air, tearing through Boardman's neck and cracking into the downed cedar behind him.

Boardman gags, regarding Rayford in dismay, his neck spouting, pumping red gouts across the white ground. He topples forward, his face crushed into the snow, bleeding out. Rayford sees the feathered shaft sunk into the cedar, and moaning, the moan rising into a shriek, he is on his feet, running, his rifle forgotten, fleeing along the rim of the ridge, the slain man falling behind.

The guttural bleats and grunts stay with Rayford, he hears them in between his own short, high screams, the animal noises keeping pace with him from across the draw. His sunglasses are lost, his eyes riven, he sees forms over there, slipping through branches, the undergrowth, he is already out of breath, out of reserves, tripping, staggering, clumsy in the snowshoes, both working loose.

The call of the buck, the grunting, the bleating, becomes the trill of giddy laughter. Rayford's snowshoes are clownish, almost sideways, he trips a final time, tumbling down the slope of the draw. He scrabbles for a handhold, plowing two swaths through the powder and coming to rest at the bottom. Snow cakes his face and clothes, he raises his upper body, lungs heaving. He is staring toward the sky, the trees once opposite now looming above. The boughs of a pine stir, pockets of powder sliding loose.

The animal sounds, the giddy laughter has ceased. The pound of Rayford's breath, his heart, shake the stillness.

In the boughs, a figure is taking form.

Branched from one arm, an alien device, two dull metal limbs that brace pulleys, cables. The man is hooded. One eye blinks from behind a tubular sight.

He is gripping a compound bow at full draw.

Rayford gapes up at him, discerning the path the broadhead arrow will take. Light winks off the chiseled serrations of the blade. He has heard about the chisel's durability, cutting through hair, hide and bone, the instant hemorrhaging of vital tissue.

It wasn't like his life flashed before his eyes, or even random images of things noteworthy. All he really had time for was to hope the arrow would be accurate and the kill a quick one.

*

Their camp is crude but sheltered from the wind. A canvas tarp and walls of logs form a lodge, cinders showering upward from their hot fire. There are three, two bristly, one full-bearded, all in rough winter garb. The barren slopes of the alpine surround them, they stand at the blaze, limbs and cones crackling, sharing a glass pipe, expelling sheets of weedy smoke.

In the twilight, they are not well lit, just a glimpse of red brow or angular nose, the baring of teeth. One man has an item in his hand, not well lit either, but known to hunters. It resembles a small flute as he brings it to his fringed lips and sounds it.

A grunt, a bleat. Idle laughter.

Fresh meat roasts on a spit over red coals. In the effulgence it is possible to identify it as organ meat. Not enough to feed three men of appetite, but then, the meal is symbolic.

Searing on a blackened stick, two fist-sized hearts.

Chapter 10

Deputy Jim Ainsworth passes another endless waking night,
another long boozy slog chasing sleep, or at least chasing the lapse
of consciousness obtained by alcohol overload, and maybe that
lapse happened, once or twice, because he wakes up on the carpet
next to the bed, in his boxer shorts, the doublewide rank and cold,
the temperature outside somewhere in the mid-teens.

J.A. rears up off the floor and the room wheels. He braces
himself against the bed. It takes a while to get his bearings, and
when he is capable of motion, he throws on a robe, sways into the
kitchen and upends a bottle of water into his mouth. Unsteadily, he
assembles the coffee maker, switches it on, leans there against the
counter as the machine gasps, steam rising. The phone is clattering
like it does every morning, but he isn't ready to engage it, he is off-
shift until he feels like getting back on it, not anytime soon.

He takes his coffee into the living room and slumps into the
fat vinyl cushions of the sofa, last night's wreckage littering the
coffee table, an empty vodka bottle, beer cans, hardened take-out
leavings, a plethora of filtered cigarette butts stuffed into an
ashtray. The mug he swills coffee from has faded wording on it –
World's Best Dad. His daughter Jennifer gifted him with it when
she was at the age of hoping for the best, pretending along with her
mother that things were on the upswing, but J.A., with his
ungovernable rage at how small a station he'd earned in life,
shattered that forecast. He'd fostered some violent episodes, nights
when he got too far into the abyss, screaming and throwing
furniture, and now Jennifer hates his guts, they haven't
communicated for five years, and her mother, Barb, who is still
pretending, sits at her dinner table with her ex-husband every few
months, dread in her heart and not much to say.

He has blown-off his family, even the dog stays scarce
when he darkens Barb's doorway, and the stabbing regret and
loneliness has never eased up. J.A. grew up in Cope, joined the
Sheriff's Department out of the army, twenty years patrolling

mountain crossroads. The whole hamlet is less than a square mile, a former mining town, lumber, all of it dead and gone, but nevertheless, they are one big happy family, they are the kindred J.A. had earlier squandered. He is their guardian. But it is just a place to squat, a passage on his way down, it is worse, because Cope has a past.

J.A. himself has a past. Obscured by the vapor of time, it still trails him like some murky shadow. It doesn't pay to look back, so he keeps his eyes ahead, performing his duties – a citation for speeding, shooing a rambunctious bear away, an opioid arrest, refereeing a domestic. Waving hello to the people, communing with them, civic meetings at the hardware depot, county park barbecues, attending church every Sunday, those rock-hard pews at the God-forsaken church.

Some good has been done. Deputy Ainsworth has saved lives, he has brought the hopeless, the damaged, back from the brink. He carries Narcan on patrols and he knows how to use it. The young lady who'd plunged a lethal mix of heroin and fentanyl into her arm, found comatose. She was too pretty for dying on a dirty kitchen floor. J.A. laid her head back, peeled the plunger, slid the nozzle into her nose. He'd never done it before, but who would've known, he woke that girl up, looked into her startled sky-blue eyes, and he smiled. "You're back, darlin." He has a real nice smile, it is said, it aligns his features, erases the frown-dent between his brows. The would-be suicides, the PTSD vet he was called in on, man had a 12 gauge parked under his chin, it took the deputy half his shift to dissuade him. But in the end he did. Worth it. They wave as friends now. Thumbs up. A savior, J.A. is. He saves lives. Just not his own. In the end, he will not save his own.

When Deputy Ainsworth has shaved and uniformed, he takes up the phone and fields various complaints and concerns, doctoring himself with aspirin and vitamin c, and the dispatcher comes in over the Motorola, requesting him. He knows her, Carla works in a small cramped room behind the Mayor's office, itself a small cramped room. Carla doesn't use code, it has fallen into disfavor over plain-speak and all the spy police scanners out there know the numbers anyway. Frankly J.A. misses the 10-Code. It made communication seem an exclusive language shared by those in the know.

"Got something here," Carla says. "Caller reports Bob Gates drove by her house in a pricey new pickup."

J.A. takes notice. "Gates is back?"

"He's back. Caller got the license."

"Let's have it."

As he scribbles the number he is already guessing he's seen said pickup in town. He was cruising the street and took note of a big late-model Ford at the gas station pumps, the paint scheme blinding, two middle-aged males up front with rifles in the rack.

"Caller say what color the truck was?"

"Orange-like, is what she said."

J.A. tells Carla he will run it down, signs off. But he's already run it down. Two middle-aged males will come up missing. Gates is driving their pickup.

If Gates is back, they are all back.

*

Deputy Ainsworth, toothpick clenched in his teeth, swings down from his 4X4 and moves across the snowy yard toward John Ainsworth's porch. His brother John is five years older and has always looked out for J.A. As kids, taking on aggressors, they battled bare-knuckled and back to back, and even when they lost they won, because they were unified. Those who'd been dusted-up admired their fighting spirit and gave them ample space, that was how it had been, in a schoolyard or an alley, or later, a squabble in a bar, and to this day the Ainsworth brothers are still backing each other up.

When John Ainsworth took sick with small cell lung cancer it killed J.A. There was hope at first, there always is. The chemo shrank the tumor, John's color came back, the brothers returned to their favored trout hole on the river. But the cancer reinstated itself. Vigorously. John rejects the notion of further treatments that might grant him another year. He doesn't want the maintenance therapy, the rounds of radiation, the unpronounceable drugs. The disease is headed for the bones, the brain, one way or the other, and time is not so precious anymore, drawing it out, clinging to the tired human framework he is losing piece by piece. As John Ainsworth sees it, the treatments would not prolong his life, they'd prolong his death.

Nearing John's porch, the Deputy's sunglasses are fixed on the young man at the wood splitter at the side of the house. Cantwell, his name is, they'd had their introduction at the café. J.A. has given him sound advice to move on, but there he is, chucking logs. That doesn't sit well, and the stare Cantwell throws back at J.A. tells him further instruction will be required for the youth to heed the counsel.

Ty appears, pushing a wheelbarrow. Climbing the porch, J.A. holds up a hand in greeting and the boy nods, absent a grin, eyes grave, as is his custom when he and the deputy cross paths. When a boy himself, J.A. looked up to men in law enforcement, they were heroic, stalwart, brave. Ty apparently doesn't perceive those qualities in Uncle Jim. It is the boy's father, Wade Deal, his DNA, that has tainted the son, turned Ty against regulations, guidelines, civil ways. One day, when J.A. has the time, he'll sit the child down and inform him of the longstanding war of right against wrong, the need for justice, impress on him some moral clarity.

The deputy's knuckles club the oakwood of John's front door and it's not too long before Rayann opens it. Her hair is pinned up, she has a rag in one hand, in the middle of some kind work, and she is not especially happy to see him. He has that effect on almost everybody, it's just part of his outspoken character, he's learned to live with it, to work around it. Past Rayann, he sees his brother where he often lands, unconscious in his armchair by the woodstove.

"Can I have a word with you?" J.A. asks.

Rayann glances toward her father, steps out, closing the door behind her. She awaits the news.

"They're coming in," he tells her.

He can see the weight fall on her, the drag on her heart, but she withstands it, she is strong and her eyes are clear.

"How long'd you expect them to stay out there?' she asks.

J.A. gnaws his toothpick. "We had an agreement. I covered Wade's ass. Now they're at it again."

She speaks as to herself. "It was only a matter of time."

"Pair of sportsmen came through. Out of Bakersfield. Got gas at your pumps."

Rayann eyes him, knowing what is coming.

"They'll not be returning home," he says.

She sags against the porch rail.

"Why do they do it?"

"I don't know."

"You used to run with them."

The deputy's face closes off to her, he shifts his gaze to the woodpile. "I wouldn't say that."

They watch Cole drive the blade of the splitter into a round. It is knotty, cracks apart with a bang.

"What are you gonna do, Jim?"

"Hammer down on them," he says with severity. "Hard."

She considers the statement. They've both heard it before.

J.A. chews his toothpick. He focuses on Cole Cantwell across the yard. "What's that story? Takin up with flatlanders?"

"He's workin his way out of here."

"Picked the wrong time to stumble into Cope."

"When was it ever the right time?"

He regards her with condemnation.

"Let him go," she says defiantly. "Turn his car loose. Let him get down the mountain."

"I got procedures to observe."

"It's gonna get out of hand."

The deputy inspects her. He seems triumphant, hearing her plea, discovering she has a personal interest in the outcome.

"It means that much, missy" he says, "you can pay the fine. Then he's free."

Rayann watches him move down the steps, nothing

charitable in her expression. Putting himself further into her displeasure, J.A. stops and turns.

"And if I was him," he tells her, looking toward the intruder at the woodpile, "I'd grow wings and fly down this mountain."

She watches him stride to his truck. It riles her, the phrasing – growing wings, flying down the mountain. And J.A. knew it would. It roils sunken memories, psychic injury that splintered, that left in her a lasting fracture. The undoing of someone close, the fateful removal of a person she had never really known.

It brought what was dead and buried back.

Her mother from under the snow.

Chapter 11

Shanna Wilson shed men fluidly, whenever the spirit moved her. She retained her last name when she married John Ainsworth, she had been partial to it through two past husbands. Those unions were brief and violent, bold country boys who thought with their dicks and acted with their fists, but were still no match for the lightning storm they exchanged a wedding ring with.

Ainsworth had been amply warned, which only heightened his desire for Shanna. She addled him, her animal beauty, her willful, reckless ways, and despite the ruination he glimpsed on the horizon, he meant to have her. She didn't come from Cope stock, her lineage continually recreated itself and was wide-ranging. One week her bloodline was Russian royalty and the next Cherokee and Sicilian. Knocking into town in an Oldsmobile with a thrown rod, she claimed ancestry to Kit Carson and she could track and shoot. The Olds went no further, but she ascended, dazzling the menfolk and angering their women. She was a prodigious drinker, a sparkling liar, a spinner of webs laden with delusions and fantasies. She never stopped moving, never slowed enough to get a bead on, and that remained the case when she locked her brakes going down the mountain and went over a precipice at 6200 feet. It was sleeting. Her newly acquired Mustang nosed out over sheer air, pivoted into the cliff wall, bounding over and over, billowing snow and coming to rest in the frozen streamed of the canyon far below.

Her disappearance wasn't acted on for a few days. Shanna Wilson habitually drifted exactly where she wished but always limped home, subdued and bedraggled, and this time she didn't. They found the dark tread marks of her tires angled into the wind and Search and Rescue went down after her. It was hard going. When they reached the vehicle she was not in it. The roof was crushed, the seat belt retracted, she disdained using them, and her body had been ejected somewhere on the way down. The snows were deep. They had to wait until spring, almost summer, before the melt allowed a closer investigation. But the team scouring the rocky walls never found her remains. The mountain consumed her.

As an afterthought, the Department of Transportation installed a heavy-duty guardrail at the thirty-mile-per-hour curve Shanna Wilson sheared loose from. Rayann thought it a poor monument, an impact resistant state-issued grave marker with no one immediately under it. She was nine when her mother leapt the firmament and invisibly returned to it, her lost bones sinking into the compounds of the underworld.

There was no funeral for John Ainsworth's lost wife, just pious condolences, and an exchange of knowing, or even vindicated glances between those who had predicted disaster. John went into the cave of himself and dwelled half-seen thereafter. He abandoned his aspirations, his well-battered but undying hopes for lasting love and happiness, and in the dispirited progression of the years the invading cancer found easy harbor and began dividing itself.

Rayann remembers Shanna as a heady shock of shapeliness and flamboyance, but pathologically headstrong and capricious as the wind. At a very young age, the daughter learned she would never be a replacement for the mother's preoccupation with herself. "It is well established I'm untamed," Shanna told her. "An alfa she-wolf. Your daddy knows better than to try to keep me locked up."

Still, Rayann loved Shanna enough to serve her. Their bond pivoted on the daughter filling in for the absences of the mother – cooking, cleaning, laundry, keeping things on schedule – a form of slavery Rayann dutifully entered into if the family was to stay afloat. She ironed her mother's blouses, carted out her bottles, silenced the dog when she tripped home at dawn. On a balmy day, they might sit together on the swinging bench under the shade of a poplar, Shanna taking the stage, embroidering reality with her rapid-fire monologs.

"I was born on a lunar eclipse. When the full moon falls into Earth's shadow, and I do have that witchy side to me – life cycles, earth, air, water, fire. I'm fire if you didn't guess. My god is a goddess. Venus. Beauty. Does what she wants and goes where she will. Had a husband who disagreed with my magic. I didn't harm him, just neutralized him. Shred his driver license in the disposal and from then on he let me be."

Shanna nudged her daughter, as if they were two of a kind. Her voice was like honey and whisky, her hair was that color, thick and lustrous, the breeze tangling it. "He claimed I had a drinking problem. I got no problem with drinking – it helps you forget the night before. The night before has to do with men in general."

"Watch what they try to plant in you," she cautioned Rayann. "It's not just their seed, it's their hungers, their failures, their fears." She grinned slyly. "Bring it on, boys. I'll have some of that. It's called control. Driver's seat. It's where you want to be"

Shanna saw that Rayann wasn't entirely following her, tapped her knee in apology. "That's just me, hon. I don't have an off switch." Then, as if suddenly remembering something, she ended the afternoon with no further words, sashaying off.

She watched her mother leave, sitting alone on the swing as it slowed to a stop. The driver's seat she mentioned would be prophetic.

Rayann packed her father's lunches in a brown paper bag and he grew mortally tired of peanut butter and stale bread but never let on. She was his only child and in his spare way he revered her, a precious gift with her mother's lines and few of her faults. If Rayann displeased John Ainsworth, he fixed her with a cautionary stare but never took her in hand. His daughter was more mature than his wife had ever been and rarely misbehaved.

Rayann loved her father without compromise. On bad days he was morose, on good days merely taciturn, but quietly, persistently, he instructed her, encouraged her to learn and grow, to find confidence, to master what was at hand, and she never doubted he held her central in his heart, that she was fastened to him. She lived for his smile, scarce as it was, when it broke the bristle of his face she was flooded with well-being, assurance, that all would be put right. When she felt lost or sad, he was not afraid to hug his little girl, his embrace circling her like a fortress. He smelled of long days, oil and smoke, and a warm, burnt scent, the salty fumes of his own humanity rising from his pores.

John Ainsworth worked in the gas station ten hours a day, six days a week. A constant man, the dedicated keeper of the pumps and the lifts, the machinery, the parts and tires and tools, but he would never come to any monetary gain. He'd started out as a mechanic in the garage. When the opportunity arose, he expended his life savings and bought the franchise. It seemed a shrewd move, but the realities of an independent operator made themselves known. His take was pennies per gallon, and there was no convenience store to generate profit. He repaired and serviced vehicles at a good hourly rate, but lacked steady business, and when customers couldn't quite manage the tab John put it on their account, often a charitable contribution on his part. A supplier, a fixer, a benefactor, his gas station was the only game in town, but for twenty years it was on the verge of going out of business. Ainsworth wound up where he started, just getting by.

At the age of seventeen Rayann married Wade Deal, a mating viewed warily by all concerned, and soon delivered a son. Ty was a fat, healthy infant, tenderly mothered, and John Ainsworth was enchanted to serve as his grandfather. He was less enchanted with Rayann's husband. Wade Deal was ten years her senior and had done time. Wild and unrestrainable as a youth, he would grow into a surly felon, his presence upsetting, hazard rippling from him. The prudent took care to ease by. Rayann regarded Wade with caution, but something magnetic drew her, he was well-built and rugged and took command. Ravenous as a wolf in winter, he capitalized on the spark he saw in her eyes and quickly made a meal of her. Much to her father's regret.

And in the next few years, much to Rayann's.

The new family moved into a three room cabin at the edge of town. From the start, Wade was scarce, and when he barged home he expected to be waited on. Rayann performed her household duties, worked at the gas station, brought the boy up, and understood she had fashioned a cage for herself. She was not Wade Deal's wife, she was his property, bought for nothing, and reminded frequently of her place. "I own you," Wade advised. "Don't buck me." Her place was as another possession, alongside his rifles, his hunting bows, his beat-up high-lift Chevy, his favorite boots. She rejected the arrangement and met with Wade's wrath – mental and physical – systematic punishment designed to snap the will and spirit. He ruled by force and fear and was provoked by his young wife's s refusal to be dominated. In the face of his violence, Rayann stood her ground. He could throw her across the room and she would spring up, snarling. Bruised but unbowed.

Getting loose of Wade Deal would be harrowing, and it would only be temporary as long as she held his son.

Chapter 12

Pulling the tow truck into the gas station, she senses his presence even before he fully appears. Rayann feels the day darken, and across the lot, his muddy high-lift quad cab pickup rumbles up to the pumps. He has come down from the mountain. Nothing good could attend it. Her insides frost over, staring toward the truck.

He turns the engine off, eyeing her, a crack across his windshield splitting his face in two sections that don't quite piece together. Rayann knows he can sense her discord from fifty feet away. She knows it pleases him.

His features are roughhewn, his jaw stubble. His eyes are a color close to black. When they latch onto something the pupils seem to project from the sockets, so pointed are they. He is busy knifing Rayann with those eyes, and doesn't turn to the person coming out of the office until he stands below the driver's window.

It is Cole, who has walked into the space between them and won't easily walk out.

She sees the driver register this new presence.

An outsider.

Wade Deal's stare slides back to her. She hasn't moved, watching him, pinned in her seat.

She sees him add it up.

*

Cole Cantwell passes a greeting and waits patiently below the truck window. The pickup wears its mud and grime proudly and he is getting sized up by this hard case with eyes rigid as agate and apparently he isn't passing inspection. He can keep standing there waiting for the request or he can shortcut the whole thing and ask what is already obvious. So he does.

"What do you need?" he says, affably enough.

The driver takes him in, tapping a can of smokeless tobacco on his knee, packing it.

"Need to reconsider. Eradicate the whole fuckin deal."

He pinches a wad of tobacco, his stare on Cole, who has the sudden sensation of leaning over a deep lightless hole, his grip on safe ground precarious. The man is extreme. With his language and the way he scans Rayann in the tow truck across the yard, Cole is ninety-nine percent sure he is face to face with Wade Deal.

Cole's reply is intended to unweight the present atmosphere.

"Start you out with some gas?"

Wade Deal slides tobacco in his lip, fixed on the tow truck. "She put you to work?"

"I'm temporary," Cole says.

"Yes you are."

Cole stands back. Across the lot the tow truck starts rolling. He and Wade Deal watch it turn into the alley and clatter away.

"Hell of a tow driver," Wade Deal says. "Seen her winch a van up from a gully and not leave a dent. Where she winch you up from?"

Cole deflects the jab. "Winched up on my own, I guess."

Wade's eyes cut to him. Flat black.

"You gonna gas my truck or what?"

Happy to look elsewhere, Cole turns to the pumps. "What octane?" he asks, and Wade Deal works his dip, his jaws flexing. He doesn't like questions. "The fucking 91."

Cole opens the pump. He swings around with the pump nozzle in his hand and the rear window of the pickup comes in full view, the rifle slung on the rack featuring itself. It triggers a jolt, the elaborate scope, the glossy walnut and blue steel.

Wade Deal, arm on the door, is aware of all that transpires in his proximity. He is aware of Cole, what he has just discovered, that his mind and his heart are leaping.

He ejects a stream of tobacco juice.

*

At the Cope Café, a local couple, looking displaced, quickly exit the front door. The snow lining the walk is dirty, the plate glass window steamed. There is movement within, the blur of patrons, three men in a booth who cannot be clearly made out.

Inside, the air is heavy with griddle smoke, Althea crossly moves through it, hoisting a tray. She delivers three heaping plates to the men slung in the booth, wilderness men, shaggy, odiferous.

"Althea," Wade Deal says. "You are a sight. Slingin hash all these years. When you plan to retire yourself?"

"I am retired. This is a hobby."

They fall to eating as the plates hit the table, packing steak and eggs into their gullets. Of Wade's two companions, Royce Dixon is the fun-loving one, his cackle loopy and his eyes off track. Bob Gates has the beard, almost a foot of black broom straw, the individual himself dark, creased as boar hide. Althea pours more coffee, all three enjoying the fact she loathes them.

Beyond their booth, others are at breakfast, all very much minding their own business.

Coming through the front door, Deputy Ainsworth.

Wade has a pint, pours whiskey into his coffee, his attention on the Deputy. Althea totals the check.

"Anything else?" She regards Wade stonily.

He grins up at her. "The pleasure of your smile."

"That you won't have."

She slaps the check down, walks off to Dixon's giggling. Gates snorts, shoveling food. Wade Deal slurps his loaded cup, cautioning him.

"Careful there, Bobby. Gettin some of that in your mouth."

"Beats them round cakes you make at camp."

Dixon frowns over at Gates. "He makes a *nice* gallet."

"Flour and water," Gates grouses. "Prefer green meat."

"Still movin," Dixon agrees. "Fresh stud-buck backstrap."

Gates bolts food without pause. "Put a Big Fifty up that ball dragger's ass."

"Love the fifty-cal Sharps. Mountain man shit."

Wade Deal interrupts them.

"Look who's airlinin over."

They follow his gaze. The deputy is moving up, customers at the counter, the tables, fastened on him. He stops before their booth, nods a cold greeting. "Here you are. Always an occasion."

The chewing stops, the three men staring up.

Wade says, "Not to worry. We keep our usual low profile."

Deputy Ainsworth isn't reassured.

Gates' beard parts. "It's just that we get so fuckin lonely out there," and Dixon lifts his throat, issues a low wail. He looks up at the deputy, his crazed eyes dancing.

"Makes you want to howl at the moon."

There is idle laughter. Jim Ainsworth indicates he wants a seat and the three grudgingly make room for him. He removes his Stetson and leans in, voice low.

"I know what you've done. The outside comes in on this, I will not cover you. I told you last time, another incident, we are through."

Wade Deal sits back, eyes wide.

"We're just honoring tradition, officer. Respecting pioneer ways. It gets a little thin up our way. We get that grease hunger, you know. That mountain is very dangerous. Trespassers are wise to double back."

Deputy Ainsworth keeps his voice even.

"You're a gang of bonepickers. You should be sentenced and executed for your crimes."

"That's harsh, J.A." Dixon says. "We strive to operate at a high level of sportsmanship."

He raises his brows comically.

"J.A. is the law here," Wade Deal reminds Dixon. "He takes his job serious. Always snoopin around, trying to string them clues together. Got that magnifying glass."

Deputy Ainsworth skewers him with his stare.

"Tellin folks, *better watch that tail light. No huntin out of season.* They'll say to him – *well, they do it, J.A. That pack up there. They hunt out of season.*"

The deputy is steely. Wade slurps more coffee.

"And J.A., he'll look at em with a straight face, look em right in the eye, and he'll say – *not that I'm aware of.*"

Dixon's merriment has a giddy tone to it, a tone heard before, from the trees across a draw. Gate's beard reveals teeth, blotched and broken. Wade Deal regards the Deputy pointedly.

"Those men were connected," Ainsworth says softly, getting to his feet, snagging his hat. "Someone will come up here. You're on your own."

Wade slouches back. "Where's that leave you, deputy?"

Jim Ainsworth turns on them, makes his way toward the café door. He doesn't know how many customers might have overheard the conversation, but there is no one present who hasn't closely observed it. Private matters are hard to come by in Cope.

*

They walk out of the café looking for Deputy Ainsworth and see him in his 4x4 down the curb, his wipers clearing powder from the windshield. He stares out at them as they clamber into the quad cab, parked between two other vehicles.

Dixon and Gates sprawl themselves in the interior and Wade keys the ignition. The engine booms into life. He checks the space he has forward and rearward and scowls.

"Kind of blocked in here."

Dixon issues his loopy laugh, Gates, deadpan, in back, braces his arms against the rear of the front seat.

Wade works the shifter, stomps the pedal.

The big tires fling snow and ice, the truck roars back, sledges into the smaller, much tidier pickup parked behind them. The force punches the grill in, headlights burst, the pickup skids several feet rearward. The passengers in the quad cab are rocked, Wade grips the shifter, Dixon howls as he throws the truck forward and stoves in the trunk of the car ahead.

Metal caves, tires grate, Wade's engine bellows as he shoves the car ahead. Diners rush out of the café, some shouting angrily, down the curb Deputy Ainsworth has alighted from his 4x4 and is stomping through the crust toward the scene.

Wade Deal hardly bothers to mark his approach. He reverses the quad cab, and with plenty of room now, wheels ahead, his exhaust blatting, drowning out Dixon and Gates in full-throated celebration.

This is what Ainsworth sees last, Gates watching him through the rear glass, dark teeth showing, the pickup's back end sliding out, throwing slush into the air.

J.A. halts, the truck dwindling on the icy main street. Quiet filters back in. Snow drifts. Bystanders watch him, assembled at both sides of the street. Their eyes are somber, their faces well-known, the citizens of Cope rendering judgement.

"Called on to perform his duty," one says.

Another joins in. "Left us defenseless."

Deputy Ainsworth moves to his vehicle.

Cole Cantwell stands among the onlookers, all silent witnesses as J.A. climbs into his truck.

Never looking left or right, he bends the front wheels, makes a U-turn and drives out of town the opposite way.

Chapter 13

The Zelda Hardrock Mine, located on the granite heights above the hamlet of Cope, is one of many thousands of mines across the Sierra Nevada range abandoned over the 19th and 20th centuries. Hardrock mines were drilled, hammered, gouged and blasted into networks of tunnels through given mountainsides. They were treacherous enough when operating, closed down they became deadly. Contaminated run-off, bottomless vertical shafts, hazardous equipment in ruin, poisonous gases saturating the air.

Gold was the object of half the mines then in existence. There were various methods of obtaining it, placer mining, hydraulic mining, but hardrock mining was the method that killed the most men. Miners who knew the ways of hardrock, the Cornish, the Welsh, were imported to carve their way along quartz veins loaded with the yellow ductile metal and many are still buried under cave-ins, or rest bonily in the arsenic-laced windings of lost passageways. Gold mining in any of its forms removed the faces of mountains, razed forests, packed riverbeds with lethal tailings, flooded towns and farmland, and infiltrated the atmosphere with toxic chemicals, devastating the American west.

In 1943 the Zelda Mine and many others were closed down by War Production Order as non-essential to the WWII effort. By that time the quartz veins were tapped out anyway and the Zelda operation was left as it stood. Situated on private land, the owner blocked the entrance to the tunnels and shafts with a massive pair of iron doors. Decades later, when the Office of Mine Reclamation made a field visit, they inspected the rusting doors, solidly in place, the tamper-proof locking mechanism, and were happy to see that further effort would not be required in remediating a hazardous excavation.

The side–by–side iron slabs sealing the mine are secured by huge hinges bolted to an iron frame set into the rock. The locking system shields a hardened steel padlock. Once keyed, the doors are designed to swing outward, as barn doors would, and it requires considerable strength to do so. In the ages the doors have guarded the mouth of the mine, only a select few ever saw them open – the property owner who installed them, and when he died, successive holders of the key that sprung the lock.

Wade Deal is the current key holder. With reserve, Macchus Deal consigned the key to him and spoke no further on the subject. Wade was then eighteen, had passed the test of manhood, a skilled and ferocious young hellion. In the flare of acetylene lamps, he explored the depths of the Zelda, the spilled carts on log trackways, the seeping ceilings and floors, fallen cables, decaying machinery, the caves, the channels, using ropes when the walls got tight, worming his way into blackness. He choked back claustrophobia, gripped by scaly stone, clambered down shafts plunging to the abyss. He trekked the arteries of the mountain and found at its heart what legend had told him would be there – a crosscut at the end of a rail bed, its hoard long concealed.

The Zelda mine is sited on a plateau. Flung across the slopes below are the ruins of a toppled stamping mill – rusty crumpled metal, the corroded block of a steam engine, a spill of great shafts and gears from an ore crusher. This detritus currently snares the light of a bonfire flaming from the rim above.

It is dusk. Wade Deal stares into the blaze, his eyes reflecting anti-social thoughts, though the gathering this evening passes for a social event. Dixon and Gates are with him, and several pickups are parked beyond their pyramid of fiery logs. Voices float through the woodsmoke, locals, hangers-on, waiting for something to happen.

The three at the fire pass a bottle of tequila, nearly empty now that it comes back around to Wade. It doesn't improve his mood. He is an unsparing man, drunk or sober, and Gates is sawing on about how his father had struck it rich placer mining. It is a worn-out story, and the sums grow on each telling.

"Placer nuggets," Gates affirms "This was up on the Trinity. "Said one month he panned out enough grams to make a troy ounce. Three-thousand dollar payday wasn't unusual."

"Fuck placer," Wade growls. "With your ass in the water

all day. Hydraulic, you pipe down the force of the river, aim the nozzle, blast away the whole fuckin mountainside." He upends the empty bottle and flings it over the rim.

Gates peers at him, dark of face. "River's contaminated," he says. "Fuckin sulfuric acid. Fuckin mercury."

"Get you a drink of that," Dixon drawls, "you be walkin and talkin real funny."

Wade does not evidence humor. The alcohol hasn't lifted him, only delivered a brooding, violent outlook. Amid the boozy talk that drifts across the evening, one large-framed youth takes the occasion to swagger up to the fire and drop a suggestion.

"Hey, Wade. Why don't you take us into the mine?"

He stands there with a half-smile, something he's conjured to make him look daring. "Sure like to see what all you got inside there."

Wade doesn't bother looking his way. His mind is on the icy crystals tumbling from the sky, jeweled by the flames, hissing softly as they pile up against the ground.

"Snow hides a multitude of sins," he observes.

The youth's smile wavers. "What's that?"

Wade's eyes veer to him. "It's what the Pastor said. Snow hides a multitude of sins. Some things need be buried. Should not be seen in the light of day."

"I'm talkin about the mine, Wade."

The steel of a hunting knife is suddenly at his throat. Wade Deal hasn't even seemed to move and his stout carbon-steel nudges the youth's jugular.

"Talkin about the mine," Wade cautions, "is exactly what you should not be talkin about."

"*I'm good with that.*"

Dixon and Gates watch the youth from across the fire, neither man inclined to offer assistance. In the shadows around them, others have ceased their horseplay, still and intent.

"Bring it up again," Wade tells the youth, "I'll dress you out like a goddamn deer."

The edge of his knife brushes the youth's throat and draws

a line of blood, superficial, not the killing cut, a slash that would sink effortlessly through flesh until it struck spine.

"Okay, man. Okay..."

Gates says, "Looks like a overgrown baby, don't he?"

"Crapped his diapers," Dixon says.

Wade lifts the knife away, delivers a hard kick to the rear, sending the unfortunate into the dark. There is no hooting, no talk, the onlookers alert, anxious to stay in favor.

He leaves the fire, ambles to the rim. He enjoys the silence held by all, it has a reverence to it, in his opinion, richly deserved. Hitching his thumbs in his belt, his gaze sweeps the peaks across the way, the valley below, king of all he surveys.

He stares into the gloom below the mountains, dusk passing in the forsaken hamlet of Cope. The last tinge of copper filters from the sky, darkness squaring over empty streets, decrepit storefronts, the sorry dwellings where no hint of light gleams.

Lastly, the church and its tilted cross are taken, leaving Cope in the grip of an enduring black frost, another Godless night.

Chapter 14

Woodsmoke piles from John Ainsworth's stone chimney, the sky above gathered, an interval between storms. It is Cole Cantwell's final day at the woodpile and he is glad of it. They are done with the splitter, he and Ty wheeling it down the driveway when Wade Deal's pickup crushes its way to the curb. His stare from the cab cuts across the yard. The event cancels any cheer Cole harbored that morning. He and the boy worked well together, laying in next year's supply of hot-burning fir, they were stacking the last of it. Now Ty disengages from the work, from the present, he is lost to Cole from that moment on.

The baritone of the exhaust ceases and Wade alights from the truck. Ty stands suspended, but Wade isn't focused on his son. His tone is aggrieved as he crosses the yard.

"You're *here*, too?"

Cole keeps his eyes on him, has no response. Ty heeds his father's every motion. His taut attention reminds Cole of what holds Cope together – fear and blood.

Wade issues his son an order.

"Come up to the house, boy."

Ty sprints for the backyard.

On the porch, Wade bangs on the front door. When it opens, John Ainsworth, stern, pallor gray, confronts him.

"You know you're not welcome here."

Wade's gaze is black. "Bring her up front, so I don't have to sully your domicile."

Rayann appears behind her father. She looks on Wade as she would something mangled. He has the aura of a bad accident.

"I'll handle it, dad."

"He's trespassin," Ainsworth says. "I'm within my rights if I shoot him."

Wade is unmoved, glaring into Rayann's eyes. "Do what she says, oldster. Be quick about it or my patience will fail."

Ainsworth's frail frame shakes with anger.

"Fuck you, Deal."

Wade swings his glare to him. Rayann takes her father's arm, silently urging him to go. Ainsworth, unafraid, willing to do battle, defers to her, glowering as he retreats.

"Old John don't look too well," Wade observes.

Coldly, Rayann steps out to the porch.

"That's because he's dyin."

Wade stomps snow off his boots, the boards under his heels shuddering. "Well, goddamn. Get it over and done."

He indicates Cole, who rests against a woodshed post.

"That your latest suitor?"

"He's doin some work for me."

Wade eyes him. "I'm debatin whether to walk over and rip his head off."

Rayann stands hating him, her arms crossed defensively.

"He's no harm. Why are you here?"

"Came to see my boy."

The front door swings inward, Ty making himself known. He has picked up his bow, his hunting rig, wanting to impress his father, gain his favor, his respect.

"Here he is," Rayann says. "You see him. Now you go."

"You intend to smart-mouth me?"

Wade motions for the boy. Ty walks onto the porch, searches his father's face for some sign of recognition.

Wade regards the bow he holds.

"How old are you now?"

"Eleven. Just turned."

"So how come you got that plaything in your hands? That toy for wimps with no upper body strength? Couldn't tap a strike with that at ten yards."

Ty, downcast, looks on the bow. "Macchus gave it to me."

Wade snorts. "Well, he should've gave you the real deal. A recurve. Wood. Bowstring. Haul back on it. A man's weapon."

Rayann speaks out, weary of him.

"He's a child. He just told you his age."

"Old enough," Wade says. "Come here, boy."

Ty scoots closer.

"You haven't met me lately. Let's hear what you think."

The boy's thoughts fly loose of him. "You look somethin fierce, Wade. And you smell awful. Like a dead bear."

Wade Deal weighs the words, gives a few deep grunts.

"The little man speaks his mind."

He drops down before Ty, ragged, powerful, his features hard and scarred. His black eyes rove over his son.

"You're sturdy," he says. "Strong bones..." He snaps his fingers before the boy's face and Ty reacts instantly, coiled, sharp.

Wade says, "I think it's time."

Rayann pulls Ty back, safeguarding him.

"You're out of your mind, Wade. This boy will have nothin to do with you. He's not growin up like that. Visit is over."

Wade Deal, undeterred, remains crouched, keeps the boy in his iron stare. "Would you like to get out there with us? In the back range? The high country?"

The boy beholds his father, the gravity of him, the lure of the world he proposes.

Wade says, "Old Man of the Mountain is up there. Taught us some things. We're a wolfpack, boy. We run down our kill. We live raw. This life here..." He scans the house, the yard, his view falling on Cole, watching from the woodpile.

"This life here, it's soft, worthless."

Ty, clutching his bow, looks on him, repelled, enthralled.

"Is there really an Old Man?"

Wade's immovable gaze holds him. He merely smiles.

Rayann regains the boy.

"Get out of here. Just stay out of our lives."

Wade Deal rises, not releasing his consuming stare.

"She knows," he tells the boy. "And she's scared. Scared of what's in the blood."

He steps back.

"When you're ready, you make your way up the mountain. We'll find you. There you will become a man."

He leaves the boy reeling, clears the porch, walking toward

his truck.

     Cole hasn't moved from the shed, gauging him.
In afterthought, Wade turns with some advice.
"Enjoy yourself. Life is short."

Chapter 15

In the basement, night fills the window well and Cole Cantwell is busy hanging a damp change of clothes on a piece of rope strung above the furnace. The sheet metal throbs steadily, he has come to think of it as an old dragon, fire in its belly, resting in its lair. Light leaks from an overhead fixture screwed to a joist. The bulb is weak, radiating a sulfur-colored glow that leaves much in shadow.

The day has not gone well. The accord Cole had built with the boy, with his mother, has been casually violated. He has an ill feeling, one of foreboding. Wade Deal has walked right over John Ainsworth, Rayann, absorbed her son, and Cole has been singled out. He is unnerved, a collision is coming, it is crucial he steady himself, summon courage and surmount what lies ahead.

On the face of it, he is outmanned and outgunned. A death-defying act is called for, and he's performed a few of those. Big Mountain, off the headwall, taking to the frigid air over an impossible spire of granite to loft down into the untracked powder below, fully intact and alive. That kind of cliff drop served its own reward, after the gut-wrench, the risk, the biting, weightless descent, there was elation, he was grounded, secure once again. In the clash that is looming, he could end up not on the ground but somewhere beneath it.

If he could flee Cope, slip away never to return, leave the few he'd come to know to their lives, to their fates, would he take that road? He was no stranger to the path of least resistance. Sandra would affirm that. His mother certainly. He ponders this, examining it very closely, hanging a flannel shirt he'd wrung out onto the rope, and then she comes down the stairs.

"Can I come in?"

He looks over as Rayann steps in. She wears a quilted nylon jacket, a white woolen cap, neatly put together, her hair braided in a ponytail. He is surprised to see her, and her appearance is welcome.

"Please," he says. "Absolutely."

She moves into the yellow light. He inhales the scent of fresh snow. She is as clean and cool, not cold, but contained, on a mission. Cole leaves his makeshift clothesline and attempts to host.

"Watch the webs," he says. "It's not the Hilton."

She's looking at the galvanized tub he left on the floor, the ribbed board in soapy water. "Laundry day here," he explains. "Althea lent me the washboard. I cleaned my clothes much like the pioneers of yesteryear. Can I offer you a seat?"

There is only the cot. She eyes it doubtfully. "Maybe not."

Cole faces her. "Are you okay? I saw what went down today. You need anything?"

Rayann waves it off. "Hey. Got some good news for you."

"Lord. I'm waitin for some of that."

"We're releasin your car. You can pick it up, fill the tank, and be on your way." She smiles up at him.

"You're happy," Cole decides. "Or it's a brave effort."

"Thought you might be, too."

"But how'd this come about? Thought I was in arrears."

"That fee has been waived." She dips into her jacket pocket, places folded currency in his hand. "Here's your wages."

Cole considers the money.

"Your work is done here," Rayann tells him, and she isn't smiling anymore. "You should leave before we get another storm. You should leave tomorrow. Early."

"What's going on, Rayann? Did you do something?"

She regards him openly. "Like what?"

"Like pay the impound?"

Her expression remains the same.

Cole's question is answered. "You are amazing. And now I'm indebted."

"You don't owe me a thing."

He stands close, studying her, or drinking her in. She knows his intent, keeps her footing. She says, "It'd be best if you were gone when Ty gets up."

"He'll be disappointed."

"Nothin new there."

"I can't do that."

She reads the moment.

"Don't be an idiot."

He leans in, meets her lips, heat flaring, her desire matching his, a hunger for convergence, a fusion of themselves, what composes them.

And all the reasons against it flood in.

She pulls back from him.

"What?" he asks.

"If I have you, I have to trade myself. I have to loosen my grip. I have to be unwise, impractical."

"Do those things."

Rayann breaks the embrace, both left unfinished.

"I'm condemned to live out my sentence. You'd never make it here."

"No judge or jury ruled that."

"Leave, Cole."

"Rather not."

"I want you to leave."

He releases her, thwarted.

Reining her emotions in, Rayann turns for the stairway. She glances back remorsefully before ascending.

Cole stands fuming, her shadow withdrawing.

Silence, the interminable night, returns.

Chapter 16

In the spread of dawn, hoarfrost feathers the Pastor's office window, casts it in a heavenly hue. He is at work in that light, hypnotized by his desktop screen, when Cole Cantwell stops in the office doorway.

The Pastor ceases poking his keyboard.

"Your journey beckons?"

Cole enters, wears his backpack, skis and poles on a carrier strap over his shoulder. He places two twenty-dollar bills on the desktop afloat with disorganization. "Hope I wasn't much trouble."

The Pastor summons a quote. "Man is born unto trouble as the sparks fly upward."

Cole grins. "I like that."

"The book of Job. Where will you go?"

"I'm not sure."

The Pastor concurs. "How can we know?"

"Right," Cole says. "Can I leave my gear by the door? I'll be back for it once my car is running."

"That's fine."

No further observations are made. They regard each other with nothing further to say.

"Well. Thanks again." Cole makes to leave. He turns.

"Just wanted to ask, are you angry about something?"

"Is it evident to you?" the Pastor asks.

"Kind of."

Behind the lenses, the Pastor's orbits are sunken.

"My ministry."

Cole's response is uncertain. "Well, it's off the beaten path. Doesn't mean –"

"In it's heyday," the Pastor interrupts, "the congregation was never more than twenty. Today, sporadic terms it best. A stingy flock. Not free with their enthusiasm. Tight-knit, they are. Mountain roots run deep." His brows close. "And darker doings."

Cole wishes for a diplomatic escape, but the afflicted gaze

of the Pastor pins him.

"I am their shepherd. Overseeing the eaters of the grass. I am ordained. Sober. Righteous. Attending to the needs of the spirit. The births, deaths, baptisms. Weddings, funerals and family counseling. Peddling broken gospel day and night. Always ready with a psalm."

"Not sure what you're getting at," Cole says.

"The hardware store," the Pastor goes on, "the post office, the market – all my pulpit. I prayed with Eunice Trager in the canned goods isle yesterday, asking God to banish her breast cancer. I requested that with a straight face."

Cole is transfixed, has no way to stop the abrupt baring of a man's soul, the wreckage glimpsed therein.

The Pastor opens his hands. "How in God's name did I end up here? It is well you ask. After my good wife departed, the Lord counseled me. *For who despises the day of small things?* My heart grew small. I sought a similar venue. No other church would at all do."

His gaze drifts, recalling cobwebbed times. *"Hello, Jesus?* I said when I stepped inside. The roof leaked, the floors were rotten, swifts nested in the rafters. Their guano was plentiful. *Yoo hoo? Son of God? Are you present?"*

He cups his ear, hearing nothing.

"We are as Protestant as they come. Sunday sermons, the congregation cloaking themselves in scripture. Lots of white space out ahead of me. White faces. That sunless early-settler skin tone. The pale frontier." His attention tracks to his computer. "Oh, there's an ant. They like to run across my keys." He flicks it off. "A few brown folk fleeing Catholic ways. One black man. Quincy. White bristle, yellow eyes. He neither smiles or speaks. He takes a solitary perch in the pews and whether inspired sermon or just plain bad, it doesn't change one particle of his life."

The Pastor shifts his glasses to Cole.

"Though tiny and worthless, I am here to serve. God dearly loves nobodies. The anonymous. The forgotten."

He seems done.

Cole is thankful. He says, "Being pretty hard on yourself."

The Pastor stares straight ahead, not at Cole, but back into himself, the cell of anguish he exists in.

Cole hefts his skis, has no final words. He nods farewell.

"It's good you are leaving," the Pastor says.

Cole pauses in the doorway. The image of the Pastor behind the life raft of his desk, the celestial light, those glasses framing his wounded eyes, is indelible.

"Satan does exist. He is here in Cope now."

*

Cole Cantwell treads over the slush and ice on Main Street, free of the stale church, breathing in the bladed mountain atmosphere. It is bracing to see the gas station ahead, to know his car awaits him, the snowy road down to the valley beckoning. He is leaving Cope behind, also what he most values here – the woman who sacrificed herself for him, who cut off any chance of her own rescue.

He understood Rayann's motive as she broke away from him. She assumed his safe passage as her task. And Cole Cantwell, master evader, is slipping out of town on her dime. He is thinking as he nears the gas station that if he had one more look at her, there in the office, or at the wheel of the wrecker, he would abandon everything, fight for her, and she would receive him. Could they somehow be blessed with fortune, stay clear of the hazards ahead, elude the forces out to destroy them? He is thinking about what it would take to reshape their destinies, if it is possible to become other than what they are, then the ragged exhaust is stacking the air, the big tires slewing through the snow behind him, all such thoughts seep away and he is left with the battered quad cab as it rolls aside.

Dixon and Gates, seated front and rear, gladly anticipate an interlude of diversion, Wade Deal drives, pacing Cole's stride. His stare ranges rudely over him.

"Goin ski touring? A little off-piste, are we?"

Cole wants to avoid a conversation, but it isn't a selection.

"Call it what you want," he says. "I'm on my way out."

"That's not even arguable."

Wade looks to his crew. "See how they are? Things get a little narrow, they turn tail, dash for cover."

Dixon looses lazy glee.

Wade says, "Those your wheels in Ainsworth's yard there? That Su-bar-oo?"

"Yup. Those are my wheels."

Dixon has a suggestion. "Race down the mountain, Wade."

Bob Gates speaks from the open window of the back seat. "Think you could outrun this old piece a shit Chevy?"

His teeth, black holed, appear from the broom of beard. Cole gathers it is a grin, looks ahead.

Wade Deal is combative. "Bob just asked you a question."

"Sorry," Cole says. "I didn't get that."

Wade glowers, Dixon says, "He got shit in his ears?"

"Question was, think you can outrun my truck?"

Cole has little choice but to look the truck over. He itemizes what he sees as they move along the street.

"Okay. It sits way up there. High center of gravity. The bed is loaded down with all kinds of crap. Is that how you're gonna run it? I see rust-through in the rockers, no doubt the frame. Don't know what kind of mill's under the hood, but probably vintage GM, which you can only build so far. Not a high-winder..."

He has stalled the trio, their stares narrowing. He knows he is about to take a dangerous leap, but it doesn't stop him.

"All that in mind, yeah, I think I could outrun you."

Gates blinks, very still.

"Ho ho," Dixon proclaims. "You hear that, Wade?"

Wade forestalls an impulse to violence, almost as if he were harnessed. He brings his stony features across the span of the seat and Dixon flattens back to let him through.

"You familiar with mountain roads, bein from down-valley? Have some experience in the slippery shit?"

"I've slipped around on it." Cole says.

That creates another stir. Wade guns his engine.

"It's on. We'll be waitin when you start your way down.

Give it your all."

Dixon chortles. "Loser buys lunch."

Wade boots it, tires spin, throw muddy snow. As the pickup pounds away, Cole sees the trophy rifle in the rack, reminded that the previous owner is no more.

He has made a bad bargain. He is from down-valley. They are not. There is only one road off the mountain. However the day works out, he's already forfeited a landing on safe ground.

Chapter 17

John Ainsworth knows about most everything that goes on in Cope and this is a matter of course. He never engages in gossip but he hears plenty of it. His gas station serves as a satellite to the local goings-on – a centrally located set of eyes and ears – and what he doesn't have a lead on, his brother J.A. fills in. In John Ainsworth's omniscience, rarely is he blind-sided. The downside is that every-day occurrences in Cope aren't very interesting. Unless a tragic event takes place – catastrophic fire, grievous injury, sudden death.

The return of Wade Deal and his wolfpack covers all three.

Strangers in Cope always have potential on the interest meter. A visit from the new guy with Fish and Game is not especially gripping, but the recently stranded young man from the flats is out of the ordinary. Cole Cantwell has conducted himself respectfully, touched a few lives, Ainsworth's daughter in particular. He is daring, willful, Ainsworth sees that in him, it goes with the youthful territory. Combine his proximity with Wade Deal's, the needle skips off the meter.

But the odds against Cole Cantwell prevailing are great. Wade Deal is a low, gut-churning son of a bitch, but he is also a warrior, one without any equal that Ainsworth has ever seen. For years he's wished for someone, a champion, to rise up and vanquish Wade. He has watched strong men from Cope fall, watched his brother Jim fold to Wade. He has taken up the mantle himself, stood that ground, and by doing so called in ruin.

In their marriage, Wade Deal liked banging Rayann around. She never told her father, but one day John Ainsworth caught sight of the injuries on her arms.

"That doesn't go," he said.

He picked up his deer rifle and left the house. She couldn't stop him. He caught Wade unloading his truck at the cabin he lived in with Rayann and Ty. Wade eyed him as Ainsworth jumped from his vehicle and approached, rifle across his chest.

"You rough up my daughter again, I will shoot you dead."

Wade welcomed the warning. "Or die tryin."

"You should leave before it gets that far," Ainsworth told him. "Haul out what's yours and go into the mountains. You're not fit to be with Rayann, or any other decent human being."

Wade spit off to the side, eyes dire.

"I'll take you up on that."

And so he did.

Before Wade Deal left for the wilds, he splashed the cabin with kerosene and torched it.

Flames burst into the night. The cabin was engulfed before the volunteer fire department could get to it. At dawn, Rayann and her son stared out over black rubble, smoking ash.

John Ainsworth was already a sick man. The damage that he'd brought down by confronting Wade Deal made him sicker. Heartsick. A few years earlier he would have gone to the alpine and stalked Deal, silently tracked him, waited for a clean shot, but he was no longer equipped for that kind of contest. He'd been sentenced to the sidelines and thereafter, when Wade and his pack made their sorties into town, he stood by helplessly – as J.A made ineffectual attempts to restrain them, as the occasional passer-through went missing, as the inhabitants of Cope, terrorized, turned their lights off and darkness ruled.

Ainsworth rolls a battery charger out to the impound yard that morning, intending to avert a crisis. Rayann has presented a handful of cash she can not afford to part with in exchange for Cole Cantwell's freedom, or at least the freeing of his car. His daughter has bravely said her goodbyes, but he sees into her aching heart.

Cole is waiting at the open hood of his Subaru. Ainsworth clamps the charger cables onto the dead battery. He turns some dials and Cole gets behind the wheel and turns the ignition and the flat-four cylinder chugs lit.

Ainsworth unclips the cables, drops the hood. "Better come up to the pumps and fill that tank," he says to Cole. "Won't see another gas station for a while."

Cole nods, his jawline tight. Ainsworth contemplates the descent ahead and likens it to a funeral, the little sedan a metal coffin, and not a fancy one.

"You won't outdrive em, son. Don't care what you're in. That truck has more torque than a tractor and sticks to the road like a leech. Those boys been tearin up and down this mountain their whole lives."

Cole squints tensely at him, conveying he already knows that, and that he doesn't want to hear it again. Ainsworth leans over the driver's window, makes himself closer and clearer.

"Ray likes you. And she's gotten very selective. Ty seems to behave around you. Not much in life has gone their way. They'll lose more. Just don't want to see them lose it to your stupidity."

His words are taken in. He stands back.

"I don't say that you can change anything. You got no stake in what goes on here. But you leave the mountain on that road, you will never make the highway."

Cole stares ahead, turning things over.

"I'm terminal," Ainsworth says. "But you need to think about an easier way to let them down."

He takes the handles of the battery charger, begins away.

Cole addresses him from the window.

"Where would I find Rayann?"

Ainsworth stops, looks back at him.

"You might start with her Jeep."

Chapter 18

Deputy Jim Ainsworth carries a Glock semi-auto on duty, a pistol that can rap off seventeen well-placed rounds in a firefight, but the gun he favors is his Smith and Wesson Model 686+. The six-inch barrel tames the recoil, it chambers seven rounds. A hefty piece, you would not want it dragging on your belt all shift, but the 686 has personality. Renowned for its reliability and accuracy, J.A. can pin a three-inch group at 15 yards. There isn't an official firing range within fifty miles of Cope, which brings J.A. to a box canyon outside town, a dry bed of rubble ending at a rock wall. People who can't afford the fees at the landfill, or don't bother with the landfill at all, come to the canyon with their cast-offs and over the years a worthy collection of residential and industrial junk has been carted in or released from the cliffside above.

What Deputy Ainsworth likes about the junk is that he can single out responsive targets, perforate discarded appliances with star-shaped holes from his hollow points, explode a row of jugs and bottles sweeping past his gunsights. Today he is decimating a ratty sofa, the stuffing bursting, until he is firing on an empty chamber. Snapping the cylinder open, he speedloads fresh rounds, emptying the cylinder again. The 686 never misses, never wavers, until his enemies lay vanquished – Wade Deal, Dixon, Gates – all three of them blown to ragged foam.

The crack of the gunshots cease, leaving the day abruptly absent of any sound except J.A. smoothly casing the revolver. It is therapy, shooting the Smith and Wesson completes him, enables him to come to terms with himself. He is not a bad guy, not at all, and he is no coward. He handles things professionally, he controls them, because he does not let others' actions direct him, it is Deputy Jim Ainsworth who chooses the time and place.

Driving back into town, J.A. decides on mid-day breakfast at the café where he can lounge out in a booth and own some food, but those plans are interrupted when Carla comes in over the Motorola.

"Hey, Jim."

"Yeah, Carla"

"We got an OD. Woman unresponsive. Roommate called it in. This is the Tyler place. Ambulance delayed."

J.A. knows the address.

"Been there once or twice. This opiate induced?"

"No one's saying. Don't want to get arrested."

J.A. slows, making a U turn. "On my way."

*

The Tyler place, when J.A. gets to it, is a shake-sided duplex that has undergone countless tenants and been put to hard use. The front door is standing open and a nervous tattooed man wearing only boxer shorts and a leather motorcycle jacket abides in the cluttered driveway awaiting the arrival of life-support.

The deputy breaks from his truck, Narcan in hand, advancing on the entrance. "What did she OD on?"

"I don't know. I was –"

"Cut the crap," J.A. says. "Coke, meth or alcohol, Naloxone won't do anything for her."

"Maybe smack," the man says as the deputy brushes past.

The doorway leads into the kitchen. J.A. sees the victim face- up on the floor near a table and an overturned chair. He kneels over her, peeling the little plastic plunger out of its container. She is still breathing, barely, her hair swept across her face. Supporting her head from behind, the deputy clears her hair and slides the nozzle into her nostril, pressing the plunger and evacuating the spray into her sinus. He waits for a response.

Her eyes flutter open. They are sky blue. She peers up at him and he is struck by the symmetry of her features. She is wearing herself away by drug use, but she is still young. J.A. thinks she could come back to what she was, under the right supervision, and with personal commitment. He thinks that because he knows this girl, he's saved her before, sprayed the Narcan into her brain on the same dirty floor, knocked the poison right out of her receptors. She came to life then as she does now, as though just awakened from a nice nap, unaware, as innocent as newly born.

She gazes up at the deputy. Rock-steady, heroic, J.A. greets her with the same words as the last time.

"Welcome back, darlin."

*

Her name is Hazel Clay, which he thinks strangely old-school, he'd expected something more defiant, like Blaze, or Rebel. She is upright and speaking lucidly when the paramedics arrive and they take her to the county health clinic. After she is examined, the deputy gives her a ride home, during which she speaks not a word. Home is the duplex where the whole thing started.

It doesn't seem like a great idea to throw Hazel Clay back into the same environment that nearly killed her, not once, but twice, and J.A. tries to express this when he noses into the driveway. His headlights shear tubs stuffed with household items, a car sitting on its axles, broken furniture, or maybe all this is an ongoing yard sale.

"I don't see any lights on in there," he says as Hazel opens the passenger door. "Is your male friend at home?"

Hazel pauses, halfway out of the truck. "He's not my male friend. He's my daddy, and I don't mean an old fuck like you."

The deputy processes that, the naked hostility. "Well, he's taking very poor care of you."

"That any of your business?"

"Listen, girl-child. Your habit of going comatose has made it my business. Did Daddy even follow up on this?"

She glares over at him. The answer is obvious, and she's as uncooperative as a feral cat.

"I got my own Narcan," she says. "I don't need you."

"You have Narcan? Where is it?"

"I got a prescription."

J.A. shakes his head. "The prescription won't save you. You need the medication on hand."

Hazel dismisses him, is out the door, slamming it closed.

J.A. watches her stalk into the duplex. A light goes on.

The deputy stares at the orange-lit window. This constitutes the intervention. No outpatient, no detox. They wrote an RX and sent her on her way. Because the behavior isn't going to change, but maybe next time someone in the room can squeeze out some revival spray. Except she hadn't even bothered pick the Narcan up. That's where Deputy Ainsworth, public servant, comes in, running around cleaning up after the those who won't care for themselves.

J.A. swings out of the truck and walks to the front door. He raps on it and stands waiting. There is no movement so he raps on it harder and presents himself.

"Deputy Ainsworth. We're not done, Hazel. Open up the door."

After some time he hears the latch and the door gaps open, her face visible. She is sullen, waiting for him to say something, and squaring his shoulders, he does say something,

"I have a sworn duty to protect the public, of which you are one. Due to your negligence, I was called out here. This is not the first time I've brought you back from the dead. So I want you to think about that. The path you're on."

Far from thinking about it, her eyes are hard, going over him, like he is some kind of imposter, like he is play acting that he is a cop, and not doing a very good job of it, which makes him angrier. He wants to shock that sneer off her face, he wants her to recognize his authority. He wants her to fucking thank him for saving her goddamn life, *twice*. Maybe he goes too far with what he says next, but she needs to hear it. She needs to understand that he has devoted his life to making right what is wrong. She needs to admire him.

"Now," Deputy Jim Ainsworth says, "my job runs twenty-four hours a day. I'm first on the line, holding off the bad guys, all the bad things, all the horrendous shit that people don't want to think about. Because it's out there. It is out there, Miss Clay, and if you're careless it will bury you."

He feels warm, even though the thermometer can't raise past 22, he is sweating under his shirt. Her eyes, he realizes, are not filled with the sky blue wonder she expressed on her recovery, both her recoveries, when he had suavely welcomed her back to the world. Her eyes are the color of gray stone, nothing girl-like held in them.

"I'll just leave you with this," the deputy says. "I'm solo out there. I am solo, I don't have a partner, a safety net. I'm all alone, Hazel. It's a long haul. But it doesn't stop me from —"

"You're insane."

Hazel spits her conclusion, closing the door on him.

He stands on the porch, stilled in mid-sentence. He hears the lock engage, the light in the window vanishes. His breath is white haze, a meager ghost dispersing in the frigid gloom. He searches his mind for a way to salvage the night, but in the end he just notifies her that he is leaving.

"I won't take up anymore of your time," he says.

Then the long walk from the porch to the 4x4, the climb in, the clunk of the door closing. He doesn't start the truck for several minutes. He is thinking if he delays leaving, her window might light up again. That having reconsidered, she might swing open that door, fully reveal herself, part child, part woman. Acknowledge his work. Acknowledge him as a man.

And the night gets colder.

Chapter 19

The road down the mountain is recently plowed, shaved down to a few inches of packed snow interspersed with dark slicks that can suddenly slide a vehicle off the embankment and into the tops of the trees. Wade Deal knows how to cross the glaze, skate over it, as do Bob Gates and Royce Dixon. They can identify black ice coming up and navigate it at fairly high speeds. More important, they have learned where the black ice is likely to be and where it isn't. That is their high-country legacy, challenging the conditions of the mountain, besting adversity, betting their lives on their prowess.

The quad cab is thunderous coming down the gorge, exhaust crashing across the snowy landscape. Racing through the switchbacks and hairpin curves is accomplished in series of controlled slides. Gates and Dixon cling to their respective seats as Wade Deal tosses the big pickup around, power-sliding is the only way to swiftly cut a corner. His passengers brace as he charges into a tight radius, wrenching out the handbrake, the truck slewing sideways. It looks like a collision until he goes full throttle, tires clawing, gaining traction. Wade twists the wheel back to center and they are off on another straightaway. No one else on the mountain can drive like that.

They pull into a chain-up area where they can watch the roadway and tag Mr. Down-Valley when he sneaks into view. To pass the time they unlimber their archery equipment. A family in an upmarket sport utility watches them from their windows. They are parked along the shoulder and deem it time to move on when Wade Deal brandishes his recurve, nocks a broadhead, takes careful aim and sends it into the roadside sign for the hamlet of Cope.

The arrow cracks through the flat metal and streaks away, the letter O in Cope obliterated.

Gates readies his compound bow. "Least you hit the sign."

"Follow it through," Wade says. "Crank up that silly fuckin

mechanism and let it do the work for you."

Gates is strapping a bow release on his wrist. "Accuracy and distance, two things you ain't got."

"I wanted that O, motherfucker. That is the bullseye."

Gates grips the bowstring with the release, draws back, eye to the tubular sight. His broadhead settles on a strike point.

"The O in Elevation. Call it the bulls-hole."

"Coined a word," Dixon says.

Gates unleashes his arrow, the road sign metal bangs out. The three study the results.

Dixon whoops. "Bulls-hole. Sure enough."

Gates sizes up his target through the cracks of his eyelids.

"Un-disputable."

Wade Deal steps in. Bare-fingered, he bends his bow back full draw. His forearm is corded, he uses no sight, just stares along the arrow shaft.

"Like to feel the weight build up. I'm holdin back seventy pounds." He settles his aim. "You got a cam holdin your shot. And a metal hook instead of your fingers."

He releases, the arrow vanishes. Everyone sees it reappear as it tears through the same hole Gates has made.

"Goddamn," Dixon says.

Wade lowers his bow. "Nothing further."

Gates glowers, eyes ahead.

"I still like the compound."

They wait at the pull-out another hour, and become inconvenienced as the snow drifts and the route from Cope produces no contender in a blatting Subaru. A rancher piloting a pick-up pulls in and starts to chain-up, then thinks of a better location when he focuses on the three wild and armed men watching his every move.

"He lost heart," Wade Deal says, watching the pickup fade.

"Who wouldn't?" Dixon says.

Wade moves for the truck. "Talkin about the flatlander."

They watch him step up into the cab.

"Let's smoke him out."

*

The Cope Market on Main Street occupies a two-story brick edifice built in 1899 and deteriorating ever since. The building houses most of the hamlet's infrastructure – the grocery, a hardware section, a counter for the post office, and municipal offices upstairs. Cole Cantwell has been tracking Rayann and this is where he finds her Jeep, parked in the side lot facing the wall.

He pulls the Suburu into the next space, beneath washed out signage painted on the bricks a century ago – Uneeda Bisquit. He is intent on standing before Rayann, but he doesn't know what he is going to say, or how the outcome that awaits them can be changed.

He finds her with a basket on her arm, working her way along a shelf of goods, checking prices, and he is struck by this woman all over again, her frame, her harmony, the way she balances herself. Her steadiness. He is at the end of the aisle, waiting for her to look his way, and when she does, her pupils widen, as do his, it feels as good as coming home.

Cole indicates the surroundings. "This is versatile."

Rayann drops a bag of coffee into her basket, watching him, assessing his next move. "Oh, yeah. They fit it all in here. Mayor's office is upstairs. Cubicle, more like."

She stays even, but as he nears, he sees some strain at her eyes, the shadow of hardship.

"We hardly see her," she continues, allowing Cole into her perimeter. "Short, wide lady. Doesn't like to interrupt the Shopping Channel…"

He is close, intent on her, the idle talk falls away.

She says, "You never left for home."

"No."

She looks him over. He feels her desire, her despair.

"Then you're still an idiot. That was your last shot, Cole."

Cole removes the basket from her hand, sets it aside.

"I ran into them this morning."

Rayann regards him, foreseeing calamity.

"Your dad gave me some wisdom," he says. "I need to think about a better way to let you down."

"Is that what you're workin on?"

"It's a start."

"Well, better hurry up on it. Think I'm gonna stand in this aisle all day?"

With that, they merge, weld together. They forget where they are, wanting to strip each other of everything, find the core, the depth of themselves.

A box dislodges from the shelf, hits the floor. She pulls free of him, breathing hard.

Cole tries quieting her.

"This is how it is. This is what we have."

Rayann stares into him, saddened.

"It's too much. And it's not enough."

*

Still, they hope there will be a way, some form of rescue, undying love lifting them above the fray. They talk of escape, a dash to freedom through the backcountry, but the backcountry is Wade Deal's country, his wolfpack claims it, nothing gets past their outposts, clears their traps. They weigh their chances, measure how thin their margins are, how frail their future, and before they are even clear of the Market they meet a deafening white burst and understand how short they will fall.

The explosion rocks the air, shakes windows, levels shock waves along the street. They see flames reflected in plate glass, dumfounded customers, and rushing outside, they see the Subaru engulfed in sheets of fire and black fumes.

Rayann grabs for Cole as he starts toward the inferno, the searing heat stops him anyway, he can't get near the car, the molten force of it blowing outward. The fiery combustion eats paint, fabric, steel, poisonous smoke piling high.

Through the smoke, Wade Deal's quad cab becomes visible, parked a short distance down the street. Resting on the prow of the brush guard is a gas can. Wade and his crew are assembled nearby, smoking, watching the excitement calmly.

Cole's glare singles him out. "He doused my car."

Wade effects his ice smile, his death's head leer. Cole's chest heaves, craving his destruction.

"What's it gonna take?" he asks Rayann.

She holds her ex-husband darkly.

"Ain't seen it yet."

*

At the Zelda Mine, another blaze composed of great logs. A sweep of red cinders ignites murky air, the elongated shadows of three figures pitched across the ivory ground.

It is a private gathering, only themselves. Their purpose is to spike terror, finalize their rule. They are there to seize the mountain, all that falls below it.

The howling begins, claiming the darkness.

On Main Street, unlit, empty of traffic, the savage discord of their throats floats in with the frost.

Smoke drifts from John Ainsworth's stone chimney. Pale in the gloom of a dormer window, the boy's face.

From his attic room, he studies the distance, the black walls of the mountain where the red of their fire flickers. Their wild cry carries into the crown of the sky, clear and cold, into the infinite.

It raises hair. That song. That call. It opens in Ty Ainsworth a longing to join the night, to flash through columns of timber, leap deep drifts, a fearsome two-legged boy-animal. He longs to scream from icy peaks with the voice of a beast.

And now a new howling comes. A wailing off from another height. It is a solitary discontent. A deeper song. Grizzled. Ancient. Piercingly, inconceivably, alone.

The boy stares out, electrified.

The Old Man of the Mountain.

This howling evokes the granite ranges, the upheaval of tectonic plates, wilderness carved with canyons where water has forged the earth apart. It evokes raw survival. What seizes flesh with raked canines. What eats bone, white vapor clouding from serrated jaws. Entrails steaming on blood-bright snow.

The howling from lower on the mountain, from the blinking fire, has ceased, the night given over to the elder voice pitched from the black summit.

That cry trails off.

Silence pervades.

The boy's eyes stay lit, even as night fills them.

Chapter 20

John Ainsworth's workhorse wrecker is an International rollback with a twenty-one foot deck and a twelve-thousand pound winch. He'd finally upgraded from his first wrecker, a GMC hoist truck built around the time of Eisenhower's inauguration. Rayann grew up with the GMC in the weeds and learned to love the industrious clatter of the International. When her father was diagnosed, she was willing and able to take towing duties on. Ainsworth is proud of his daughter, her skills in the art, geometry and social dexterity of roadside rescue.

Speeding to a call, Rayann smoothly shifts the seven-speed transmission, never knowing what the next alert will entail, except that it's a good bet she'll be greeted with anger, misery, remorse, or as an angel of salvation. She once extracted a Ford Falcon from a man's living room. He'd been reading his newspaper when the car came to a stop inches from his Lazyboy and he was overjoyed to see the celestial tow driver step in. On a bad day, Rayann removes the aftermath of surface-to-surface contact – a basic rear-ender, or a horrifying marriage of humans, polyurethane, plastic and steel.

Today, her first job is not challenging but is nonetheless grim – hauling the burnt-out husk of Cole Cantwell's Suburu onto the deck of the rollback. He is present, watching her work the winch, his mood somber. On reflection, his journey started out with a majestic sweep, now the mountain walls are closing in.

When the remains of the car roll into place, Rayann shuts the winch down and they regard each other.

"Where you want to go with this?" she asks.

"He's not done."

She agrees. "We can call it in, but we're off the beaten path. It'll take time to get someone up here."

He blinks at her. "We *have* someone up here."

Rayann strips off her gloves, warning in her eyes.

Cole says, "Don't we?"

*

From the exterior, Deputy Ainsworth's manufactured home bespeaks a certain pride of ownership. It is an older model but the paint is kept up and the surroundings maintained. A trim green yard emerges in the spring with a stone pathway across a grassy expanse to the porch. A steel shed in the rear shelters neatly stowed tools and a John Deere lawn tractor. The deputy parks his state-issue 4x4 under an attached carport, and that's how Rayann and Cole know he is home when they pull up.

Inside the doublewide there is no claim to tidy appearances. Unkept and unloved, this is the dank burrow of a mournful man. The walls are barren, Jim Ainsworth is not inclined to decoration, and there's not much worth displaying if he was. Low light or no light is his preference, he doesn't need a brighter look at the fake woodgrain peeling from the kitchen cabinets every morning, nor does he want to ponder the dark discolorations on the nylon carpeting from solids or fluids of unguessed origins. It is better to dwell in the fuzzy glow of the yammering big-screen, daily, nightly, where he can sling himself onto the swollen sofa, sink into the scuffed Naugahyde and explore semi-consciousness.

On this morning he bears unshaven bristle and a depleted level of energy. His health is dragging. He is not a smoker but he's been walking around with mold in his lungs, a green cough that clings to the lining of his chest and won't be shaken loose. Lit against the big-screen is a skyline of bottles and cans stacked on the coffee table, whatever he's been slugging down recently, there is a drink even now in his hand, and he honestly doesn't know if it is day or night. It's easy to lose track on sick-leave with the shades tightly closed. There is, however, an interruption gaining his attention, an insistent chiming mixed with the noise from the over-boosted TV.

He looks to the doorbell. Somebody calling for J.A.

They stand at the threshold awaiting him, and it takes a fair amount of time for the deputy to show up. There is a neat white railing of molded plastic and a plastic chair with twelve inches of snow on the seat. The wind is up, dusting white spray across the yard. The cold spears them, their purpose here is not heartening. Rayann is unable to smile when Jim Ainsworth finally hauls open the door.

He stands in dishevelment, peering out at his niece and her companion, whom he has no liking for.

"Look who's on my doorstep," he says.

Rayann takes him in, it's hard not to wince. "Thought we'd stop by," is all she says.

The deputy reviews Cole Cantwell unsociably.

"You bring an outsider here?"

"He's pretty much a resident now. Gonna ask us in?"

Cole has no desire to enter, nods to Rayann.

"I'll wait in the car."

J.A. allows Rayann inside, closes the door on Cole retreating toward the Jeep. He shuffles to the sofa, drops into it with a rubbery squeak. She regards the mindless din of the screen, bracing herself.

"Mind if I turn that crap down?"

Not waiting for an answer, she finds the remote, cutting the sound altogether. J.A., boozy, inert, watches her find a seat across from him.

"Wade torched Cole's vehicle," she tells him. "It's slag."

"Have an eyewitness to that?"

"He was smiling. Had a gas can."

J.A. finds a bottle that still has some liquor in it. "Want me to strap on my six-gun, go out and arrest him?"

Rayann follows the thin stream he pours into his glass.

"Shoot him would be better. This is a subject we've taken up before. I want to know why you're not doin your job."

J.A.'s answer is to tilt his glass, choking the swill down.

"You used to run with them. Wade, the others."

He gives her his stock answer. "I wouldn't say that."

Her gaze hardens. "Dad called it an unholy alliance."

He searches for a toothpick, his bleary eyes examining her.

"Go ahead, honey. Lay it out."

Rayann observes him, the wastage of her uncle, not kindly.

"Well, okay. I'd say you did something back-when that wouldn't be particularly good for anyone to know about. And Wade and his boys, they're holdin it over you. That on the right track?"

J.A. shifts his toothpick. "Just like a train."

"So, if you try to come down on them, serve justice, you stand to lose. Might as well pack it in."

He says nothing, the big-screen shuttling aqueous images.

"So instead of that, uncle Jim, you thought it would be better to just hole-up here. Thought you'd just kind of lay low…"

J.A. claps his hands together. "Fuckin Nancy Drew!"

"…with a wagonload of cheap booze and your daytime TV, while they take your town apart."

The deputy lurches up from the sofa, swaying.

"Where's my keys? Need some more courage in a bottle."

Rayann rises, confronts him.

"Jim, you can't stand straight. Let's get this out. I've heard the rumors for too long."

J.A. laughs drunkenly, looking at her clasp on his arms.

"Get what out, girly girl?"

"You need to clear this," she says. "Pick up your life."

His eyes are unfocused, he shakes his head. "What's to pick up? We're runnin on all cylinders. No misfires here."

Rankled, she releases him. He sweeps a beer can up, aims it at his mouth and Rayann bats it out of hand.

He is stilled. She bores into him.

"Dad knows what happened, but he'll never say. Your brother's goin to the grave with it. But you ain't dead yet. You keep this up, concealing it, lettin it run your life, you'll end up eating that six-gun of yours."

"What you doin, Ray? What in fuck you want from me?"

She faces him fiercely. *"Nineteen years ago, uncle Jim."*

"Nineteen-years ago what?"

"The couple that went hiking into the backcountry."

He finds his focus now, staring into her eyes.

She says, "The couple that went missing."

The deputy has never forgotten the couple. That memory is like an abscess in his brain.

"They were all over the news," Rayann says.

J.A. rears free of her, weaves for the door. He claws the knob as she arrives behind him.

"You were new to the department."

Deputy Ainsworth throws the door open and lurches onto the porch, then off the porch, staggering away through the snow.

He is a hundred yards out when he stops, a lost figure on the barren landscape. There is nowhere to go.

He is rooted there, gaping into the past. Rayann comes up behind him. She is persistent. "The couple that went missing, Jim. The couple who were never found."

Jim Ainsworth's shoulders slump. Rayann sees the burden of his recall, images dredged from the recesses, settling on him. When he speaks he chooses not to face her.

"They were in trouble, those two."

She waits, wind coursing through the pines beyond. Alcohol, the passage of time, have not impaired his recall.

"Inexperienced. They just weren't equipped. It was fuckin February, for Christ sake. Six foot snows. Minus twenty…"

He stops, that vile day assembling. The dark storm over the mountain. The snow tumbling, wet, heavy. The trackless silvery meadow. The phantom conifers.

The flimsy two-man tent. Half-buried, a ribbon of orange nylon snapping in a gust.

J.A. stares into that. The tent. The two children who thought it would protect them.

"They were kids," he remembers. "Seventeen, eighteen. You think you'll never get hurt. You think you'll live forever."

He rattles a cough, his own life wearing away.

"They got snowed in. He went out to find help. One of those tragic stories. Usually they walk in circles, lie down, die. This one got a little piece of luck."

He beholds depths long looked away from.

"Or he thought he did."

Chapter 21

Their objective is the magical playground of the towering Sierra Nevada, the snow-crossed country that looks like God has showered across it heaven-loads of white sugar. They leave before the sun is up, in his beater 4-Runner, bouncy and noisy but handling the snow going up just fine. Near the trailhead, they pull their packs from the truck, marveling at the shattering blue of the sky, sparkling meadow, the balsam scented afternoon. Theirs is the only vehicle in sight, promising a gloriously solitary adventure.

She is auburn-haired, wears it long, she is willowy, he had fallen in lust with her face and form. Neither yet twenty, she is daring enough to accompany a boy she hardly knows on this foray into the fabled high country.

She gazes happily into their trail through the trees, tightening her straps, adjusting the weight of the pack. "So you've done a lot of snow camping?"

He shoulders his own pack into place. "Oh, yeah." He is tall, thin, skinny really, and when suggesting the trip he somewhat enlarged the scope of his experience. He has only camped in the snow a few times, the last when he'd forgotten to pack his food supply and spent a famished two days hiking back out. His objective now is to marvel at the scenery, and that included her. He is looking to get close, very tight, and the cozy privations of a two-man tent will probably do it. She is athletic, willing, no fainting princess. He admires her spirit.

For his part, he is handsome in an unformed way, and plenty strong in spite of his bony build. He has endurance, is a runner who paces the miles effortlessly. He is a swimmer who tears up the lanes. In his constant restlessness, he never holds still, his lungs and his blood flaming away.

They wear thick gloves, ski clothes, set off at a bold pace.

"How many miles will we make today?"

He assesses the white terrain ahead. "As many as it takes to set up camp before sundown."

She gauges him. "That's kind of vague. You ever hear about the Donner Party?"

"It didn't go well. We're better equipped."

They cover ground quickly. "You're with a tri-athlete," he assures her. "If you fall behind, I'll hitch you up to me and we'll carry on."

She laughs mockingly. "No way you're gonna carry me. I go under girl power all day long."

It starts out like that, their glad rivalry, their bright energy, the trail almost whizzing by underneath them, but he is noticing that his boots are taking on moisture, his socks are damp already, and that maybe the fashionable hiking wear he'd paid big money for wasn't as ideal for snow as it was billed. The pack is heavy, too, becoming a bit of a load, and when he glances at her pack he sees how the padded straps are digging into her shoulders.

"My God this is beautiful," she says, their path cutting along a ridge, a wintry watercourse winding below.

All around them glacial peaks break the sky.

"Gorgeous," he says.

The sun is sliding behind the mountain they cross, the final burnished Sierra light bringing on further accolades. They praise the mountain, the snow-blue wonderland they travel. They become two silhouettes. Darkness slams down on them.

They have to pitch camp by flashlight. They have reached an expanse of silvered meadow between arctic slopes. They search out some flat ground and unfold the tent and prop it up with shock-cord poles. She finds rocks and makes a fire ring while he assembles the rain fly over the tent.

"This will help the snow slide off," he tells her.

"Will it snow tonight?"

"We had a beautiful day. But it changes fast up here."

They are both ravenous. He uses the flashlight to find wood, leaving her in the dark. She hears him thrashing through the trees and the night brings on a deep cold, the icy current piercing the nylon of her down jacket. She realizes then that the down fill was not the best choice, because her sweat and the snow have dampened the feathers inside, clumps hang in the jacket with no insulating properties at all. A blazing camp will be most welcome. Absorbing the flaming heat, they will fire up some dinner. They will drink hot tea, watch the comets careen across the atmosphere.

Those images warm her briefly, but can not overcome the sinking premonition that none of those things will happen. Not on this night, and not on any other.

*

The storm comes in and seizes the sky, cliffs of surly cloud limned by the dying moon. Weighty snow sleets over them. He looks like a narrow ghost, bringing in an armful of wet wood, hardly wood, elastic branches, damp roots, soft cones. She huddles there, the light swinging as he kneels at the ring of rocks, shivering, hands unsteady with his little knife, the blade peeling ribbons of damp bark, kindling no dryer than the debris to be lit.

They do not get a fire, only stinging smoke, and the ring of rocks and its debris are soon buried by drift. He pulls her into the tent, the sides heaving in the wind, the world outside muted, then dead silent as the snow cascades over their camp, entombing it. They make their two sleeping bags into one and lay fully clothed, chest to chest, arms wrapped around each other, and are no warmer, the freeze outside the tent permeating all within. She tells him to strip, and he questions that as she tears her own clothes from her, teeth clattering. Her bra and panties she keeps on, he is down to his underwear, they embrace under the padded bags, flesh to flesh, heads covered.

Hot at their center, frigid at their edges, they listen to the storm heave snow against the tent and the ridge of it begins to bow. In the deep of the night, half-dreaming of a hoary, hostile kingdom, a distant clamor comes to them.

The nature of it assumes form – a wild cry, the baying of raw throats raised in unison, shrill, demented, surging from the blackness out beyond. It opens fear in them, the volume uneven, nearing, then retreating on the wind. He thinks it is the howling of canines, she hears in it the timbre of something other, a human tone, but she says nothing. They return unsettled to their half-dreams, their polar outland. No one sleeps, but their naked heat, their exhalations, keep them alive.

Dawn comes, a pewter mist, the mountain, what grows from it or composes it, lost under the snow. It is too deep to go any further and they are no longer inclined in that direction. They are freezing, exhausted, their faces already blistering. Without fire they can't melt snow for water or heat their freeze-dried food. A question of survival has arisen.

"We have to go back," she says.

He stares through his sunglasses toward the route they'd taken in. Or what he thinks is the route. The meadow has been reshaped, heavily cloaked in white, it seems impossible to identify any sort of landmark they have passed. A dizziness shakes him.

"I don't see the trail," he says.

She falls silent, untangling her thoughts. Now she knows. She has taken the measure of him. He is not all who he said he was and they are in deep trouble. The romance, the exuberance, has wilted and the imperative is to find rescue.

"What will we do?" she asks.

He seeks courage. "Find the way home."

Her boots have frozen overnight, she can't get them on. He pounds his feet into his, rimmed with ice. He cuts a pair of staffs from pine branches, crooked things to probe the snow depth and keep him upright. He gathers food for her, uncooked meals she can gnaw. When he sets out she is not heartened, she senses he is going in the wrong direction. Deeper into the mountain.

She wants to call out to him, but she has no evidence.

She watches her savior dwindle into the whiteness and she crawls back into the tent.

*

His path meanders and it is slow going, wading through wet snow, hip deep in some places, running into hidden snags or boulders. He becomes very tired one hour out, his hooded jacket sodden, his pants hard with frost, his boots ice blocks. He can't feel his hands or feet and he isn't seeing anything that tells him he's found the way home. Snow-shrouded pines and hemlocks abide, boughed giants marking his doomed efforts. He drags past the trees and when the trees fall behind him and the snowy slopes ahead stand barren, he admits he has been going the wrong way, that he has struggled up into the alpine, the unforgiving heights of the mountain.

He has not the strength to turn around, remains in place, his hood over his face, his face frosted over, his frozen gloves gripping his improvised hiking staffs – his branches.

His breath clouds the air.

As it disperses, he sees objects out ahead, dark dots against the snow. There are four of them, moving toward him. As they grow closer, a snarling grows with them. He makes out what they are, ski machines, fast approaching. He raises his branches, waving them, screams out hoarsely.

"Here! Here! I'm here!"

The machines leap the drifts, closing in. Soon they scream up before him, slewing to a halt, white spray settling.

The sleds sit four abreast, motors pouring heat, the fumes wafting. Each rider wears a balaclava, the face, the head and neck, sheathed in black. They are clad for hard weather, observing him through goggles. He can't see their eyes.

He tries to gather some dignity, keep his voice steady. He is overwhelmed that they have arrived, but he downplays his jubilance.

"Glad you're here," he says, his mouth numb.

He feels foolish, ineffectual, before their ragged company. They are armed – compound bows, three of them, and the one without has a wooden bow slung across his back. That man shakes the sleet off himself and is the first to speak.

"You out here alone?"

He does not trust the tone, it is unfriendly, but he is in the backcountry, and these four don't look partial to social graces.

"No," he answers. "My friend's back at camp."

"Who's your friend?"

"My girlfriend," he says.

The riders glance at each other. It seems they approve.

"You're a little out of bounds," the man with the wooden bow says. They are lined up in front him with their sheathed heads and their iced-over goggles and he is trembling, with cold, hunger, fatigue. With dread. Their images waver, distort, in his fever they become black beetles crouched astride rockets.

He fights the need to collapse, leans heavily on his sticks.

"Where's your camp?" the man with the wooden bow says.

His eyes flutter closed. He wills them open.

"I wish I knew."

Among them, short laughter ripples.

"Well," the man says. "Get on. We'll find it."

He crooks his gloved fingers, motioning him forward, and reluctantly the youth labors through the snow, punching his sticks into the high crust, working his way forward.

The four watch his trials, saying nothing more.

It seems shabby, how the trek has gone so wrong, how the day has turned. His regret chokes him. He doesn't yet apprehend the proportions of what lies ahead, but he knows this much. The man with the wooden bow will blast away and he will cling to the seat behind him. The four riders will find the camp.

It will not be the way home.

Chapter 22

Jim Ainsworth stands with his back to Rayann, flakes drifting over him. He has fallen silent, his head inclined, tracking a formation of squalling snow geese on the flyway overhead. He watches the birds until they veer off over the trees, their noise dissipating.

Cole attends grimly. He would like to displace himself from Ainsworth, the sight of him, but Rayann is not done, so he remains. She holds steady, but he can see her anguish, demanding forth what she hoped never to hear.

"Let's have the rest, Jim."

The deputy stirs, breathes in deeply.

"We were out on winter hunt," he reflects. "He just fell into our hands. I was part of the pack. Not what I am now. Gallant. Respectable."

He gets quiet again.

"What happened, Jim? Tell me what happened out there."

Jim Ainsworth turns to her. It is hard to look on him, on his eyes, exhuming what he'd buried, the starkness of that day.

"We put him on the sled," he tells her. "Followed his tracks, the channels he plowed through the snow. We dug the girl out of the tent. She cried. She threw her arms around us…"

Rayann and Cole wait. He has stripped himself bare, nothing is left of who Deputy Jim Ainsworth pretended to be.

"I cried, too."

Rayann fears the worst.

"Go on."

Ainsworth stares inward.

"Go on," Rayann commands. "What happened?"

He sinks, crouching in the snow, strength emptied.

She doesn't want his answer, she wishes she hadn't ordered it, even before he speaks she is reeling, but it can not be rewound, it can't be called back.

He groans. "We ate them."

Cole is rocked, looks to Rayann. Her eyes close against the

atrocity of it. Ainsworth's soul is disintegrating. He sees the orange of their tent, half-buried. He sees the blood strewn across the snow.

"Aw God..." he chokes out. "Heart and liver. We threw their corpses down the shaft."

Wrenched, Rayann kneels by her uncle. The wind cuts her.

After some time she finds the will to extend her hand.

"It's done," she says. "It's over. Let's get inside."

J.A. shivers, her hand on his back. She peers up at Cole, who feels outrage, disgust, who at her bidding strides to the deputy, helps him to his feet.

Rayann stays behind, watching Cole guide her uncle toward the trailer. She collects herself, preparing for catastrophe, the end of Jim Ainsworth, the end of her existence as it was. The end of any semblance of innocence or order in the settlement known as Cope.

*

After a period of catatonia, pillowed on the sofa with no lights, no big screen, no booze, staring blindly into the darkness, J.A. at last summons the wherewithal to rise up and walk into the shower, which he does fully clothed. His garments stink, he stinks, it all needs to be cleansed, scalded under the hottest of water, disinfected, and when his clothes sag off him, he offers his skin. Steam rises from his chest and neck, burning a first-degree red. He grimaces, withstands the pain until the shower runs lukewarm.

He shaves, trims his nose, his nails.

It does not absolve him.

It is evening now. J.A. is sitting at the kitchen table, neatly dressed in the uniform he's knife-edged with the steam iron. Silence abounds, he is in thought, sorting out what is left.

He is ready. He drinks the last of his coffee, retrieves the phone, the landline, receiver in hand. He taps the numbers and waits patiently as the line rings. A woman answers. He greets her and asks for her husband, who presently announces himself.

J.A. says, "Hey, Captain. Jim Ainsworth here. Sorry to bother you at home... Well, I'm better, thank you. Bronchitis, I think it was. Laid me out."

He leans forward, soberly. He is going through with it, there isn't anything he owns he can't leave behind. From this moment on, Deputy Jim Ainsworth is a new man, whatever that represents, but from herein he is a different individual, earnest, broad of torso and maybe one day, after enough sacrifice, penance, acts of bravery, after pulling the plug on Wade Deal, ending him, maybe then he will find some form of redemption.

"Listen, Captain," he says. "I have a situation I'd like to discuss. Phone isn't suitable. Will you be free sometime tomorrow?"

*

A small blaze flares in a fire ring. Cole Cantwell stands at it, tilting a pint bottle of firewater to his mouth, the only name for the raw yellow-brown concoction Rayann found at the rear of a kitchen cabinet. He takes a hard swallow, extends the bottle.

He says, "Two two-hundred pound men in a three-ton truck. How could they just disappear?"

Rayann receives the bottle with gravity. Her father's house stands beyond her, the windows dark.

"Macchus," Cole continues. "His wife Ida the Butcher. The howling. Wade and his pack. The hikers who ran into J.A. How far does this go? This horror show?"

"It goes all the way back."

Cole studies her.

"Say again?"

She slugs whisky, handing him the bottle. "I said, it goes all the way back. Back to the wagons trapped below the pass. Back to the survivors living in holes in the snow."

He observes her uneasily.

She says, "It started there, and it never stopped."

"Is this like a tradition?"

"It got handed down. If you were born and raised here, you'd know what the past was and where it's kept hidden."

Cole holds the bottle to the fire light, sloshes what remains.

"You're scaring me, Rayann. You know where the past is hidden? That's kind of a big deal, isn't it?" His eyes fix on her. "How come you're just now telling me?"

"You overstayed. I wouldn't have told you at all. It's the kind of thing that can change your perspective. Not for the better."

She nods toward the bottle. "Rest of that's yours."

He finishes the rough red-eye.

"Right now," he says, "regardless of where we were born and raised, we need to think about getting the fuck out of here."

They hold a stare, dark-eyed, flames cracking.

Chapter 23

On Main Street a pickup sluices along the tire tracks worn through the snowy surface of the road, the occasional citizen passing on an errand. Lately an afternoon in central Cope is sparsely populated. It could be argued the afternoons always were, but there exists a sense of desertion, of quarantine, where formerly gatherings, though modest, were socially inclined. Whatever the limitations of a village of 200, at its best it was a compact community that pulled together when conditions turned adverse.

Now word is out. The shared and long-standing delusion that things are stable has been punctured. For the inhabitants of Cope, not acknowledging what has always lurked in their midst will no longer hold it off. Deputy Jim Ainsworth has unearthed ghastly skeletons and rendered the blind eye inoperative. His confession seems to have traveled at the speed of sound, no sooner said then heard and repeated across the boundaries of the hamlet.

It follows that when J.A. parks his truck in front of the café, many curious eyes are on him, though few watchers can be seen. It is a blue morning, a warm front has brought on a thaw. Ice encasing pine limbs or porch eaves relaxes, releasing its hold. The start of the day reflects the deputy's frame of mind – the storm has lifted, new business is at hand. Walking into Althea's he is resolved, groomed, his white Stetson hat blocked and spotless, jacket pressed, shod in a pair of black Tecovas, dress boot profile, ready for anything. He has left his service pistol behind. Substantial in its custom holster is his Smith and Wesson 686+ chambering seven magnum loads.

A gut-heavy rancher brooding over a coffee mug looks up from the counter, his expression stupefied, as if J.A. has entered from central casting – the white cowboy hat, the outsized gun on his hip. The deputy's manner is steely, until Althea comes forth from the kitchen smiling, and then he is soft-spoken, deferential, as any central casting peace officer would be in the presence of the elderly hostess.

He asks for coffee to go and Althea briskly fills a cardboard cup and sifts in the requisite amount of sugar. She caps the cup, opens the till and closes it before the deputy can extend the bill in his hand. She says firmly, "This one's on me, Jim."

The deputy nods his thanks. "Know better than to argue."

She hands him the coffee, assessing him. He seems in the act of unweighting himself, no longer bent under the harsh terms of his prolonged and self-imposed sentence.

"Busy morning?"

"Headed down," he says. "Got a meeting."

Their eyes meet. Althea says, "You take care on that road."

J.A. considers her. "Why do you say that?"

She dissolves unwanted visions. "Well, I don't know. You've been comin in here since you were a boy. Gave you your first job. A dishwasher you were not." She puts a napkin to her eyes. "It's just... I wouldn't want anything to happen."

It pulls on Jim Ainsworth's heart, her concern, her humanity. Gently, he clasps her hand.

"Only thing's gonna happen," he says, "I'll hit that traffic on Three-Ninety-Five, my aggravation's going up and my gas gauge is going down."

Althea nods tearfully, her smile weak, and J.A. overcomes her with his grin, the grin that completes his face, a wide open grin that defeats uncertainty, delivers courage.

He releases her hand, turns to the clarity of the morning outside the plate glass, the warm light banked over the assemblage of Main Street. With that light, the promise of renewal.

"Going to be a beautiful day."

Althea watches him walk out with his coffee-to-go, step up smartly into his truck, slip on his aviator sunglasses, pull away. It grieves her that she has no faith in his prediction.

Behind Cope's shaded windows, others also watch his departure. Their respective faith in him varies, but for everyone, Deputy Jim Ainsworth is their last hope.

Chapter 24

Though Rayann took Wade Deal's last name in marriage, after the marriage was sundered she was quick to resume her standing as an Ainsworth. Her son Ty did not go that way, he is a Deal, and the power of the surname cuts a swath through his school. Everyone is mindful not to ruffle the son lest they incur the wrath of the father. Wade Deal has removed himself from civilization, but even lurking at its fringes is enough to stamp a warning.

Education for Cope's far-flung sector of the county is a two-room modular at a barren crossroads, grades K-12. The boy arrives here after forty-minutes on a fifteen-passenger Starcraft that is anything but. Tired and slow, the interior is defaced by a succession of students who may not excel in English but are expressive with felt pens on a bus. The driver, hunched in his seat, has given up on discipline and keeps his eyes locked on the road.

The student body of the public school comprises thirty-two kids, outliers from neighboring farms, ranches and lost villages like Cope. As does his father, Ty Deal runs with a pack. Grady, built like a weasel, is his right hand, Myron, square and compact, is his left. Together, the three are bent on overturning any pretense of order in the tattered school.

Ty's teacher, Mr. Greenfield, doesn't like him, not at all, but he is careful with it. He is a sparse-haired man who belts his pants at the ribcage and his lessons on the American Revolution have the effect of lead, dead weight that does not stir. This is immaterial to Ty and his cronies at the back of the room, busy conducting their own subjects, foremost the anatomical properties of girls, followed by after-school dust-ups, and regularly, the comedic properties of Mr. Greenfield himself.

"Yo, Greenie," Grady calls out, posture indolent. "Could George Washington eat corn on the cob with them wooden teeth?"

The classroom barks laughter.

The levity is lost on Mr. Greenfield. "Wood was never a component of Washington's dentures," he informs the upstart. "It was not used by dentists of the time."

Ty Deal takes up the inquiry. "Sir, what did they use?"

"Well. Gold. Ivory. Even human teeth."

The classroom exclaims.

"Human teeth?" Ty says wonderingly. "Did Washington's dentures ever talk back to him?"

That brings down the house, and while Mr. Greenfield flails for control, Ty, Grady and Myron dismiss themselves from further studies and begin a ramble on the reputed loose morals of a twelve year old student named Mona, whom they hope to encounter later.

*

The prominent features on the scruffy lot that serves as the school's playground are a basketball hoop, a handball court, and a green dumpster. Ty and his pack cruise the perimeter, accompanied by admirers, feral children who flit in and out of their ranks like grassland sparrows. At the handball court, a wooden backboard on a pad cleared of snow, they find a large boy kneeling on the concrete.

"Here's Brewster," Grady announces. "Hey, big guy. Slower than the hour hand on a clock."

Brewster is more or less Ty's neighbor. "His dad's got him loadin hay bales all summer," he says. "Works him like a mule."

Brewster greets them with his wide, friendly face. He's been drawing circles on the concrete with a pencil compass.

Grady says, "What you got there, Brew-sterious?"

Brewster displays the compass. "This."

Ty says, "What you doin with it?"

Brewster smiles, big jaws, horse teeth. "Making moons."

Ty, Grady and Myron regard his work.

Myron says, "Look at that."

"Shouldn't even be in normal school," Grady mutters.

Ty studies Brewster's compass. "Where'd you get that?"

"Stoled it," Brewster answers proudly.

"From Greenie's desk?"

Brewster nods wisely.

Ty extends his hand. "Give it over."

Brewster's frown puckers his forehead. He is still kneeling on the concrete, and even then is nearly their height.

"I'll trade you for it," Ty says, fishing in his pocket.

Reluctantly, Brewster hands the compass to Ty.

Ty receives it in his free hand. "Those moons you made are pretty, Brew, but I got somethin you'll like better."

Brewster's eyes widen. "What is it?"

"This," Ty says, and as all look on, he bestows on Brewster a folding knife. Four inches, a lockback, common enough, but in the offering its polished black handle and nickel bolsters gleam gemlike.

"You give him your Buck?" Grady says.

Myron whistles. "Sweet gift."

"You take that knife," Ty tells Brewster. "You can clean fish with it, you can cut rope, or you can whittle, carve yourself some of those funny animals."

Brewster seizes the knife, seeing in his mind how he might now gain his way into a world that's always just beyond his grasp.

The four boys hold there on the concrete, assimilating what has just transpired, and then Ty slaps Brewster's back and moves on, his companions following.

"I got a drawer full of em," he tells the others, and they don't know whether to believe him.

"What you gonna do with his protractor?" Grady asks.

"It's a compass. Gonna put it back in Greenie's desk. Sees Brewster with it, hell will break loose. Brewster's old man'll whale the living shit out of him. Got a saddle whip. I seen him use it."

Lunch at school is whatever they brought in a bag, ranging from a lovingly prepared three-course meal to stale leavings from the night before, to nothing. The three of them sit on their customary bench overlooking the ballfield, under snow six months of the year.

Rayann ensures that Ty is never without a decent lunch. She allows for someone in his group coming up short and Ty usually has something to spare. That's the case now, and there's some back-and-forth about Myron not wanting to accept charity, but in the end he does, biting into one of Rayann's infamous peanut butter and jelly sandwiches, and actually liking it.

"Your mom put the peanut butter on first, or the jelly?"

"The peanut butter."

Ty is watching Grady consume Fritos. He eats like a squirrel, holding chips in his fingertips, biting at them. "You put the jelly on first," Ty says, "peanut butter slides off."

"That's what I thought."

It is another boring afternoon, until Mona, the twelve-year old they'd been discussing earlier, happens by with her own cohort, three rural debutantes pledged to her but not as spectacularly post-pubescent. A few months shy of thirteen, Mona is fully formed.

Grady expels Frito fragments. "Behold Girl-Woman."

"Oh, God," Myron says. "Here she comes."

Ty drops the remains of his sandwich.

"Can't keep your eyes off her."

Mona, her followers, want nothing to do with them. As she breezes by, Grady says, "So, Mona. I think them hormones in the chicken-fried steak really worked."

Rude laughter, the boys, not the girls. The girls scowl, their trimmed brows aslant, their violent thoughts easy to read. Mona's gaze is iron, strikes Grady momentarily dumb.

"Fuck off, rodent," she says. "Far and wide. You're still hung like a pre-schooler."

Her girls shriek in hilarity.

"Prayin for the first pubic hair," Mona goes on, to greater shrieking. Grady flushes, his friends struggling to mount a defense. Ill-advised, Ty wades in. He needs to reclaim their honor, transcend his years. Insult like an adult.

"Did they name you Mona because that's the sound you make when your grandpa sticks it to you?"

"Moan-a," Myron groans. "Moan uh, uh, ohh."

Mona reacts instantly. Ty doesn't even have time to remove

the forced grin on his face when her purse slams into it, a suede purse with lots of fringe and a silver buckle, all of it overwhelming his head. She is a strong girl, robust, the blow taking Ty off his feet and leaving him sitting dazed on the dirty snow.

Mona's girls regard this open-mouthed. Grady and Myron ball their fists, dance toward Mona, back away in a bluster that goes nowhere. And they have a larger audience, already surrounded with onlookers, students of all ages drawn to the conflict, welcoming it.

Mona stands victoriously over Ty Deal. "That's where you belong," she spits. "On your ass. You and your little shitheads with voices ain't changed yet."

Ty has never been knocked down before, much less, by a girl. He wins all his fights, even when he doesn't actually win them, when an opponent who wants to avoid the senior Deal's displeasure allows him to win. He jumps to his feet and the crowd on the fringes yell and gesticulate gaily. He has mud on the seat of his pants and his face is scarlet, bruises forming, he has very publicly been dealt with and wants to regain his standing.

He charges Mona, halts inches away. "What you got in that bag? A fuckin brick?"

She eyes him contemptuously. He is fallen.

Ty turns to the crowd. "She's got a fuckin brick in there."

Mona turns her back on him. She nods to her followers and the four embark regally.

The bystanders gape. Ty Deal is at their center, biting his lip, his eyes slits. No one openly mocks him, though there is a current of mockery present, and something else has arisen, it creases the air, an urge that is shared. A bloodlust.

The day has not been satisfied.

Ty walks from their center. Grady, Myron, uneasily meet him. He doesn't know what his next move will be, but the harmful mood is swelling, he sees the features of those gathered sharpen, he sees the savage energy in children's eyes.

At the handball court, two seniors, footballers, have someone large against the wooden barrier. They're calling out and the crowd is pouring that way. Ragged kids pound across the snow-trodden lot, shouting, and Ty finds himself moving quickly toward the new commotion. He tries to make out who they have against the backboard, the students are blocking his sight, but he already knows who it is, it couldn't be anyone else, and when a gap in the crowd opens up he identifies Brewster.

It is some kind of game. At first, Ty is unsure of the process, but the two seniors are issuing directions and a line of chattering kids is quickly assembling, trailing out from the court single-file. Ty does not join the line, he heads toward the front of it, and as the two seniors come into view he understands what the game is. They have Brewster pinned to the wood, one shoulder offered, and each child in the line takes a turn throwing a punch.

A kid in a hat with earflaps gives it all he's got, the thud, the smack of flesh, causing a cheer. Brewster is jarred, has a fixed grin, he is grinning against the pain, grinning to be a good sport. The first in line heads back to the end and the next steps up. This time it is a girl, a spindly thing, her face clenched in anger. Her fist strikes the meat of the shoulder sharply, happy shouts rising.

The seniors bear down on their victim.

Brewster's grin has no humor in it, it is just a formation of his mouth. Ty moves past him, the handball court falling behind as he makes for the modular.

Mr. Greenfield is at his desk, forking a piece of cake through his teeth. He wonders at Ty Deal's sudden appearance and Ty states his concern. They have no fondness for each other, but at least they can agree that things have gone too far.

"They got Brewster out there. Punchin him pretty good."

Mr. Greenfield seems unmoved. "Whom do you refer to?"

"Couple of seniors holding him. A line of kids."

"Students?"

Ty studies him, his unwillingness to intervene.

"Yeah. Students."

"Boys? Girls?"

"Yeah," Ty says. "Boys and girls."

Mr. Greenfield forks another piece of cake. "They're just

kids having fun. Now, if you'll resume your lunch period, I'd like to finish mine."

They hold a gaze, each seeing clearly into the other.

Ty heads outside. Mr. Greenfield is weak. And Ty is weak for coming to him. For expecting help. He is even weaker for trying to help the weak. He thought what was happening to Brewster was wrong, but that is not the way of the world. What is happening to Brewster is what is natural. What is happening to him is right. The strong eat the weak.

The single-file line leading to Brewster hasn't diminished. Instead of taking his place at the end of it, Ty Deal cuts in at the front. Students complain, shove each other. The two seniors stare hard at Ty, but Ty has his own stare. Icy. Unblinking.

Brewster, pinned there, angles his eyes.

He thinks he sees a friend.

Chapter 25

On the way down the mountain Jim Ainsworth has much to occupy his mind. Regarding the upcoming meeting with the Captain, he harbors no illusions. It will be time to turn in the badge. His confession will pull the plug on his career, his way of life. He'll be tried and sentenced in the courts, incarceration is a given. But having turned himself in, with a good lawyer, his demonstrated remorse, he could be out before long. He's been turning it over, constructing a plan for renewal, and he has never felt a greater sense of purpose.

It starts with his ex wife Barb. Her life is stable but nothing exciting is happening, nor is it likely to. She works at the post office, the locale is sparsely populated and the job is slow. She goes home to the house J.A. left behind, a featureless, cheaply constructed three-bedroom situated on a rock-strewn lot. She doesn't date, or have a man, friends are few. Their daughter has moved across state.

For J.A.'s part, since they divorced he's gotten over some bad habits – no more raging, ranting, no more flying chairs. He has learned to take things in stride. This is his first week without alcohol and he's feeling fine. Drinking to excess is no longer required. And he's been talking to his brother who runs a security company in Bishop. A supervisory position might be arranged, hastening his parole, and with the job very decent pay.

The proposition he will make to Barb is – why not throw in together? When he is released in a short period of time, why not unite again, with the mistakes behind them and the future beckoning? Start all over. He'd have his job, she could transfer to a busier station. They could remain under the ramparts of the mountains, the region each was born to and still loved. With their new outlook in place, the revival of romance is not out of the question. He thinks back to the weekends when they lingered in bed half the day. It would be fun to rekindle that. Neither of them are dead below the waist. Clean and sober, the world ahead, a paler world, but safer one, a steady path for the years ahead.

A yellow road sign indicates that a thirty mile per hour curve is not far ahead. Everyone knows it's the curve Rayann's mother drove off, the sheer drop Shanna Wilson galloped her Mustang over, meeting yawning sky, then stony cliff. When Jim Ainsworth rounds that curve he will be halfway down the mountain and that likely puts him out of hazard and well on his way.

Once his report is in, and missing persons files reopened, there will be a heavily armed detail coming up the mountain for Wade and company. Heading down, Ainsworth is prepared to run into them. They could be up in the alpine, or just as easily, somewhere downhill, where they would take an immediate interest in his approach. He has no intention of stopping for a chat if they wave him over, or even slowing down, and he has the back-up to enforce that decision. In addition to his 686, he brought the riot gun, a police-issue pump-action that looks brand new, in fact has never seen service, locked in an upright position between the front seats. It is established that staring into that twelve-gauge bore is a great persuader, and he has no qualms in presenting the business end should that be called for.

Just the same, he is greatly relieved that a confrontation hasn't coincided, that in all probability he has seen the last of Wade Deal. He has so much to do, so much to go onto, that when the filthy high-lift quad cab shoots up in his mirror, he rejects the reality of it. He does not accept the huge tire chained like a battering ram to the pickup's brush guard, dismisses the notion that Wade Deal himself is right now on his rear bumper, his accomplices Dixon, Gates, urging him on.

Ainsworth's vehicle shudders as the chained tire thuds against his tailgate. Shoved forward, his speedometer swings upward and he shouts out in real-time terror, his situation brought jarringly home. He fights the steering for control, stomps the brakes and the wheels lock, shrieking, smoking, the pickup behind him bellowing, jammed against his rear end, and then he has no steering, his vehicle skidding into the thirty mile per hour curve, front tires carving a direct path for the beam of the guardrail, the depth of the canyon beyond. Ainsworth snaps his seatbelt free and has time to fling open his door before the front of his truck collides with the ribbed steel. The guardrail bends outward, posts leaning, the truck lifts over the barrier and heavily leaves the earth.

The deputy tumbles across the asphalt as his 4x4 hurtles into the void. Deal's quad cab bangs to a stop on solid ground.

J.A. rises, dirt and debris in the air. Wade and his crew leap from the pickup. They are weaponized. The deputy veers toward a shallow gully gouged into the mountain. In his flight, he is torn, already breathing raggedly and the three are in close pursuit. He hears them wailing, on the hunt.

He is also aware of traffic going by on the road, people on their way up or down the mountain, people having a normal day, maybe wondering what these grown men are doing running into the gully, but no one is about to stop and investigate. It sickens him, that all his exertion, his desperate fight for his life, is being played out against passersbys on their mundane missions.

It doesn't take long to reach the terminus of the gully, which becomes a narrow cleft ascending a granite wall. He takes a stand at a spill of boulders, extending his 686 from the side of one. The first man coming into view falls into the alignment of his front and rear sights and he fires, the recoil contained, a burst of gravel where the man was. It's a miss. The target dived for cover.

Gunshots ring, rock chips fly, rake his head. They have taken positions along the gully. Blood is in his eyes, sweat. He sleeves his face. His heart is banging. He edges a view ahead. He can't see them, but then a fusillade from a semi-auto strikes the granite and he sees the smoke from that and he pinpoints it, cracking off rounds.

He withdraws. He doesn't know if he hit anyone. He thinks not. As he sleeves the blood from his face he thinks it a poor arrangement, backed into a wall, the sun just now breaking over the peaks, the day lost, all he wanted to accomplish. There is no going back, erasing the call to the Captain, easing into the folds of the sofa and blurring out on the big screen. The inevitable will be played out.

Gunfire thuds from the gully. He has spent six rounds and is down to one shot. He brought extra ammo, a speedloader, but those items went over the cliff with the 4x4.

Ahead, the man emerging from the brush thinks all revolvers are six-shooters and implies as much.

"That's it," he calls.

It is Royce Dixon, creeping dramatically up. He carries an AR-15. Coming in behind him, Wade Deal, Bob Gates, armed with similar firepower.

"Think we got you, Jimmy," Dixon says.

J.A. debates the use of the last magnum load. For himself? Or go out with a blaze? With all the unfit deeds already stacked up against him, it would be a pathetic memorial, Deputy Jim Ainsworth turning the gun on himself.

And Dixon, only ten yards out, can't contain himself, stutters his giddy laugh and proves impossible to miss.

J.A. frames him in the sights and knocks him down.

Chapter 26

Cole Cantwell is pent-up, itching to get moving, and he wants to have a conversation with Rayann's son. He is walking through the trees behind John Ainsworth's house seeking Ty's whereabouts because that's the area he was last reported in. Cole has taken the lead on explaining to the boy why he and his mother will be transporting him from Cope for an extended vacation, even though Rayann has not yet agreed to this assumption. Nor her father. When Cole brought up the idea of temporarily relocating, John Ainsworth delivered his flat refusal, and Cole doesn't expect Ty to be enthusiastic. They share few interests, but Cole is thinking he could teach the kid a few things about skiing off cliffs, and that might lead to a rapport.

Cole finds Ty busy in a clearing. The boy grasps a recurve bow, taking aim on something in a conifer, a squirrel as it turns out. He lets fly a broadhead as Cole walks out from the trees. The shaft whizzes away, clipping a branch in two and the fat gray rodent leaps to safety.

"Hey," Cole says in greeting.

Ty peers over his shoulder at him. A collection of small game lies slain at his feet. It distresses Cole to make out a squirrel not so blessed, a mangled raven.

"That your collection there?" he asks. "You gonna mount that? Take it to the taxidermist?"

Ty scuffs a shoe at his kill.

"Did pretty good. Damn broadhead goes right through em."

The wood of his bow is finely grained, lacquered. "Lost two new arrows out in the woods."

"What happened to the compound?" Cole asks. "The bow your grandad gave you?"

Ty regards him unsociably. "It was a plaything. Instructor helped me make this in wood shop. Recurve is the way to go."

Cole gazes on the dead animals. "Pretty cool."

"You don't think so."

He eyes the boy, who eyes him back.

"I didn't break no laws," Ty tells him. "I can come out here anytime I want."

"Sure you can. Now that you have a copy of your dad's bow, you can follow in his footsteps."

"Man, you don't get it," Ty says, and his eyes are no longer the eyes of a child. "You're not from here. This is how we live. Me. And Wade. Macchus. Royce. Bob. All them. The way it is."

"Slaughter is what it is. Nothing more."

The boy fumes. "Those things on the dirt are weak. Weak because they're dead. I'm strong. I'm the one that's still here."

He backs away, his features twisted. And Cole sees that he has confirmed himself as a misinformed outsider. Maybe he leaned on the kid too hard, because there will be no understanding. There will be no happy family.

Then Ty is running off, and Cole understands this will be his only view of him. Rayann's boy will always be a fleeting form lost in the light and shadow of the trees.

*

At sundown, the hamlet is sunk in the sable dusk and with nothing stirring the quietude is complete. On darkened Main Street, only the Cope Café and the gas station across from it are lit.

Cole Cantwell is closing up. The lights blink off and he steps out of the office. Keying the door, he hears the approach of a vehicle and identifies it through the dimness. A pit opens in him.

The high-lift quad cab rumbles into a parking spot across the street. The engine shuts off. Wade Deal drops out of the driver's door, Bob Gates leaving his side. Muddy, unsmiling, they walk into the café.

Cole, in shadow, studies the quad cab, perceiving something different about it.

There's a tarp strapped over the bed.

Inside the café, Althea comes out of the kitchen, surveys the two customers sprawled at the counter. Wade Deal and Bob

Gates are the definition of unwelcome and her expression makes it clear. They have been conversing in a slow-winded way and they cease their talk, sullenly taking her in.

Althea says curtly, "We're about to close."

"*About to* ain't a done deal." Wade advises her. He angles a pint bottle over a cup, pours a tarnished stream into it. "We came in hungry... Bob."

Gates, beard stiff, skin pitted like rind, pushes an item tied in a bloody cloth along the counter toward her.

"Have Juan back there fry that up."

Althea regards the stained bundle with disgust. "I'll do no such thing. What is that and why did you bring it in here?"

Gates, sucking a cigarette, coughs a laugh.

"Organ meat," Wade tells her, and Althea has never seen so openly his scorched and sinister presence. "Big ol buck."

He winks at her, a furrowed eye naked of any comfort. He has dark spatters on his jacket, throws his whiskey down his throat. Althea contemplates the raw thing on the counter, coming to a sickening conclusion.

Motionless in the dark of the gas station, Cole Cantwell comes to life, his intent taking him silently across the street to the flank of Wade Deal's pickup. Raised up on its huge tires, the truck bed is even with his chest, blanketed with a dirty camouflage tarp. Cole looks across the tarp to the window of the café. Althea is gone, the two men remain at the counter, their backs to him.

He looses the cord at the front corner tie-down, steps into the rear wheel rim to get some height. He lifts the tarp, slides the narrow beam of his penlight inside.

The light grazes tools, plastic bins, a gas can, settles on a length of grimy canvas. Full-bodied.

Cole pauses, his beam stilled.

The upper section of the canvas is hidden behind the bulk of a large worn tire. The lower section exposes two black boots. The toes are abraded, like they were dragged. Still on the feet.

Cole cuts the light, withdrawing.

He slides down the side of the truck bed, his blood leaving

his face, the enormity of what he's seen, the malignance, bearing down on him.

Rising from that, anger. Cold, measured rage.

Before he leaves, he looks to the rear window of the cab and the trophy rifle is there, suspended in its rack. The driver's door is unlocked. It is a simple matter. Cole stays low, they never see him, and when he moves into the night the rifle is his.

Chapter 27

The dramatics in Althea's café have left no service, no cook, no Althea herself, and the two of them get bored and tromp out. As they mount the quad cab, Wade Deal sees immediately that the rifle is missing, and Gates sees it also. They sling into their seats and Wade starts the truck, scanning the closed gas station across the street.

"Don't know where the thief is, but I know who he is."

Gates stares ahead. "The flatlander was already a dead man. How you gonna kill him any farther?"

Wade prods the accelerator. "Make him wish he was truly dead the first time."

Gates' brow dips. "I'm wrestlin with the logic."

The truck wheels through the slush. They are heading out of town, toward the hulking terrain that dominates their lives, decrees the appearance of the sun, the moon, decides the weather. That holds, in its twisting bowels, its lightless depths, a great vault of the untellable.

Gates has the bundle in his coat pocket, no prize anymore, not holding up well to travel. He suggests he throw it out the window and Wade is amenable. He watches Gates release the bulky rag into the dark wind and it leaves their sight.

"Headed to the next world, Jim boy, less a heart."

"Next world," Wade says, "is one floor down from Hell. No heart don't matter a lot."

Up on the plateau, the iron slabs barring ingress to the Zelda Mine prove stubborn, the hinges shrieking as the two men put their backs into swinging them open. When accomplished, there is enough room to admit the quad cab, its headlights illuminating the rocky passage ahead. They roll into it, the groundway flooded, the chiseled walls starkly grained.

"Smell arsenic," Gates says.

"What's arsenic smell like?"

"Stinks of garlic."

"Well, let's get this done, save your nose."

Their path into the mountain takes them into the thick of a darkness that even the high-beams fail to penetrate. In that murk Wade knows when and where to stop the truck. He jumps from the driver's side and Gates exits the other door with a battery-powered lantern. He props it nearby and in that weak light they assemble at the tailgate, dropping it open and flinging back the camouflage tarp from each side of the truck bed.

"Law enforcement will be up here," Gates mentions as they drag out the rolled canvas, full-bodied, ending at the black Tecova boots. "Give em a few days."

Wade says, "Don't have to make it easy for them. Why don't you visit that radio girl."

Gripping each end of the canvas, they swing the weight over a square hole in the ground, their lantern light glancing off timber shoring descending into the mountain.

"Radio girl?" Gates says. "Carla?"

"She's got the switchboard. Disable it. It's already loss of signal up here for mobiles. I'll take out a utility pole or two, that'll cut the landlines."

They are practiced at what will proceed, standing across from each other, positioning the tarp, releasing it on Wade's nod.

The dead air in the netherworld sucks the weighted canvas away and Deputy Jim Ainsworth's cratered remains plunge forever from sight.

Their aim is true. They stare down, and the plummeting of the corpse is only a brief slap of wind. Maybe thirty seconds pass, standing over the shaft, their ears straining for a responding sound, a conclusion.

"Assume that is a bulls-hole," Gates says.

Wade Deal breathes in the mineral reek of the substratum.

"That's the beauty of it. You hear nothing."

He moves for the truck and Gates snaps the last of the butt jutting from his beard over the square hole, the ember tumbling.

*

In the years after the vertical shaft in the Zelda Mine ceased any industrial function, it was adapted as a trash chute and used solely for removals, the permanent banishment of the inconvenient to the hot slate guts of the earth. No one knows how deep the shaft goes, it had been dug by teams of 19th century Sinkers, Cornwall men who were built like oxen and could see in the dark. They didn't keep records and later forms of measurement had not found a base where the shaft ended. The mountain ate secrets. Those dropped down its gullet were gone for good.

On the other end of the scale, Wade Deal and Gates decide to install Royce Dixon in the mountain's rocky heights, securing him to the limbs of a tortured juniper tree twisting up from the escarpment. The gnarled tree has weathered a thousand hostile seasons – blazing sun, sub-zero winters, lightning strikes that ignited redly and burned out blackly. As old as the tree is, the form of burial Dixon receives is far older – a sky burial, an excarnation.

"What happens here," Wade explains, "he will be de-fleshed by biology, his spirit released to join the cycle of life and death that circles this planet."

They are on the precipice, dragging Dixon's clothes off, as is the custom. Gates is hauling on the pantlegs. "When he last change these trousers, ten years ago?"

Wade is busy peeling layers of soiled garments off the torso. "The Zoroastrians ran excarnations," he says. "Since the dawn of history. They strip the dead to ease the transfer from man to vapor."

"That right?" Gates says. He flings Dixon's pants away and doesn't like what's left to remove.

"Europeans," Wade says, "Iron Age. They left their dead exposed. Tibet, India, Iran. Right here, the US, we got farms where donators decay on the open ground. Name of science."

It is time to raise Dixon into the juniper, and this is accomplished through strength and teamwork. "In the old west," Wade says, "the tribes built burial scaffolds."

"Seen those," Gates grunts.

"They'd sacrifice a favored mount, lash its head on, leading the way into the afterlife." Wade pauses for breath. "The warrior got arranged on the platform above. He faced the sun, the galaxy, and whatever else was comin in to take him apart."

"And there you have a variety," Gates says.

"A fuckin ple-thora."

Here on the rimrock, with the high winds a dirge, Royce Dixon's dispersal will be similar. It is a disposition of honor, though Deal and Gates have no honorary words, gazing up at the naked offering propped in the jagged seat of the tree.

"No family to speak of," Gates calls over the gale shearing the ridge. They stand against it, fur collars up.

"Buzzards," Wade says, and the length of the world from his viewpoint fills him, the reaches of the sky, the towering granite, the snowy blue-green of the canyons below. "Eagles. Badgers. Cougar. Bear. Ants and beetles. All wild for flesh. That's his family."

Gates squints over at him. "Wordy. But I take the meaning."

Wade watches above, the red-skulled turkey vultures gliding in majestically, sweeping in circles.

"They're here already."

Gates tracks the birds.

"I ain't up for that show."

Wade Deal considers him, the odd concession to decency.

"Had some fondness for Royce," Gates explains.

Wade nods, a hard nod. There is no act in the natural world he can't look upon. "Then you leave, Bob."

Gates appears offended.

Wade says, "I'll catch up."

CHAPTER 28

The Pastor commands his pulpit, the arched windows along the nave opaque with winter's stingy light. He is consulting his notes on today's sermon, the dull poverty of his surroundings challenging anything transcendent. On the altar behind him is a wooden Christ, hand-fashioned in a simpler age, the facial expression less excruciated then impatient to be done with it all. To the left of the altar is a dust-layered pump organ that gasped its last a quarter century ago and has never been carted out. As the basement furnace has no reach here, the Pastor stokes coals in a parlor stove crusty with corrosion and not far from quietus. Parishioners sitting on the left aisle forward pews find some semblance of heat.

When the Pastor looks up from his notes, this is where his flock has gathered, a handful of haggard residents squirming on creaky benches. They have come to find hope, most of them, and the Pastor aims to fulfill that need. He has donned robes, vestments worn by a predecessor, stowed away in a cobwebbed closet and shaken out. The last wearer was a larger man of God, as the Pastor has more room under the cassock than he would like.

"So today," he begins, and his voice lifts, only to sink into the soft old beams holding up the roof, "I'd like to talk about our greatest enemy, and that enemy is Satan. His attempts to corrupt –"

Loud hacking jars him. John Ainsworth rises from a station at the rear, gripping the seat back ahead of him, stabilizing himself.

He is trying to regain his breath.

"We've had enough of Satan," he manages, "We want some God today. We want some goodness. We're in the mood for some holiness. So deal it out, Pastor. Put heaven in our blood. Fill our souls. Before the last of mine rots away."

He resumes his seat, unrepentant, and Quincy, the black man with the yellow eyes, watches him gravely from the next aisle. Both are regulars, and in the Pastor's view, both have written off hope. He wishes they would just step outside and wander away, but they never do, they attend regularly and maintain their skepticism throughout. It's an ordeal, putting up with them.

"Thank you for that, John," the Pastor says. "John Ainsworth is an example of our forbears. Those hardy people who came here with nothing and made an existence..."

It doesn't sound exalted, the chalky faces trained on him, the lifeless stares. But the Pastor has a larger problem at hand. His gaze has found a man who has entered soundlessly and leans on a post at the rear. In the shadows back there, his eyes are pits.

"Those who made an existence," the Pastor continues. "Who endured and survived... Settlers of the untamed land..."

He's losing his concentration. Wade Deal is motionless, his dark sockets aimed toward him.

"They ran into difficult conditions. They did what they had to do. We do what we have to do. And that is why this place, our community, is called..."

The word Hell jumps into his mind. He leaves it unfinished. He removes from his sight the man at the rear, the unholy recesses of his demon stare. He retakes his sermon.

"This is what we're about. Renewal. Revival. Redemption."

"The three fucking R's," Wade rumbles.

All have turned to him. The Pastor holds fast to his notes.

"We abide. We perpetuate..."

"Let's hear about the carnal part," Wade says, and his words have a timbre, a resonance, they are more compelling than the words from the pulpit. Everyone is a listener.

"I'm sorry?" the Pastor says, the wrong address, as weak as the daylight in the windows. Striving for authority, he pinpoints the discourteous speaker.

"Wade Deal. Did you wish to participate?"

"The carnal part," Wade repeats. "The nasty shit. The bodily appetites. The animal nature of man."

The Pastor seeks words, all eyes on this outlaw, this wolf.

"Like Lucifer," he states, "he has been expelled from God's house, but still, he continues to violate it."

"Let's hear about the food chain," Wade prods. "Let's hear about kill and be killed..."

He eyes a woman in quilted nylon as she stands, rustling stiffly past him. He turns from her, the door closing on her exit.

"Let's hear about the sins of the flesh," he says. "Let's picture what we're all composed of. Let's picture bleeding meat."

The counter-sermon ceases. Those gathered keep silence. Particles in the smoky heat of the stove rise toward the rafters. The Pastor follows them, cindered souls called to heaven while he strives to contain the battle on earth.

"The carnal mind is an enmity against God, Wade Deal," and he is losing them, the church is emptying out. John Ainsworth remains where he sits, facing the pulpit.

Wade Deal makes his way forward. The Pastor's eyes dart like minnows caught behind his glasses.

"God," Wade intones. "Now you're gonna force me to blaspheme in church. God, Pastor, is a fat, mean, tired old whore. God, in heaven or on earth, is nowhere to be found."

The Pastor grips his notes, handwritten in that morning's light, a clear, illuminating light from the window that infused his mind, his penscript, with well-being, a serenity brought from without and within at the same time. How distant that is now.

"God is all, Wade Deal. Though we are imperfect, he loves us perfectly. Though we are incomplete –"

He stops cold, Wade warning him with an extended finger.

"I'll tell you about God," he says, bootheels bowing the floor planks. "Old Macchus left me roped to a fencepost. My collie couldn't keep the coyotes off a calf."

He passes John Ainsworth in a pew, who merely watches him, nothing more to fear.

"Macchus shot the dog, no ceremony, and when I cried, he tied me to that post, took a strap to me til he opened up my ribs."

The Pastor hangs onto his pulpit, an unsteady craft under his grip. Wade arrives before him.

"I saw three nights come and go. Frost sheeted me and I had plenty of time to ponder who was up there."

The Pastor beholds him, this unwanted visitation, a beast in man's skin, smelling of sinew, moss, the hide of trees, old blood.

"I even called on him," Wade confides. "It was the last time I used his name. Except in vain."

He awaits the Pastor, who prays for intervention.

The church is vacant of congregation. Except for the last in the pews, a disbeliever himself.

"Well, you know, Wade," John Ainsworth says. Wade Deal turns to him and Ainsworth marks him with his resolve.

"All things considered, it might've been a better idea, if way back then, Macchus had shot you instead of the dog."

In the raw silence that ensues, the Pastor fears to stir while Wade Deal's glare spears Ainsworth.

The frail man regards him calmly.

Wade chuckles.

"Not bad, Old John. It strikes me as funny."

Wade conducts himself to John's bench. He stands over him, puts a boot up on the seat, mirth, and death, glinting from his rabid eyes.

"And damn, man. It hurts, but it's true. Had the old bastard popped a cap in my brainpan instead of the dog's, we'd have all been better off."

He holds Ainsworth's steady gaze.

Ainsworth says, "I haven't heard from my brother. I went down the mountain, saw the guardrail taken out. I didn't see his truck, but it's a fair bet it's down there."

Wade Deal's lip turns up.

"You'll meet your end soon," Ainsworth says. "I'm not a religious man, but when you come for me, I pray to whatever is supposed to watch over us that it's me who gets to pop that cap."

His words find no roost. Wade runs his eyes upward, checking the web-strewn rafters.

"Pastor," he says, "You have any rope or strong cord?"

The Pastor's glasses wink from the pulpit.

"I don't know what you're asking."

Wade faces him.

"Ain't that tricky. Gonna hang Old John from your beam."

The Pastor regards him rigidly.

Wade returns to Ainsworth, who merely observes him with his tired eyes.

Wade drags his boot off the bench. "Doom closes in."

He considers the Pastor.

"Sermon didn't get off the ground," he tells him. "I'd work on that hopeless way you got about you. Maybe meet Jesus for coffee and donuts, get the man's input."

He leaves them, making his way down the aisle. "We'll meet up presently, John. You don't choke to death first."

Both men watch Wade Deal push the door open, stride out into the cold light, the sound of his boots in the snow diminishing.

After John Ainsworth departs, the Pastor furiously stokes the parlor stove, feeds it to capacity. The iron cracks as it expands, but the fire fails to overcome the frost lodged within him.

Chapter 29

John Ainsworth walks into his house with his heart sagging.
Rayann sees the damage goes deep. She takes John's jacket and
hangs it up, sits him down, puts a bowl of hot soup in front him. It
is all he eats anymore, and that hardly.

"Won't need the soup," he says. "We'll need my 30-30."

"J.A.?"

He nods. Or he could have shaken his head. It comes down
to the same result – Yes, J.A. No J.A.

They each stare into the loss, and what will follow it.

"You able to make a call?" John asks.

"No one is." She regards him steadily. "We still got Carla
over at dispatch."

Her father is not lifted. "It's comin down."

He doesn't have to elaborate.

When John Ainsworth became a widower, he ceded the
bungalow's master suite to his daughter and slept in his shop in the
garage. There was another bedroom he could have used but it was
right next to the master and he didn't want to crowd Rayann. The
shop was insulated, heated, had room for a single bed, and
Ainsworth joined his gallery of implements, power tools and
small-engine machines. He considered himself a machine, a
venerable flesh and blood apparatus powering the welfare of his
household, and he could fix anything except the mad division in
his own lungs.

Rayann received the bedroom after she had freed herself
from her marriage. The white oak floors, the built-in shelving, the
bathroom tiled in 1920, became her sanctuary, the only place that
was hers alone, and now she is sharing it with Cole.

No lamp lights them, they are silhouettes against the sheer
fabric of the window, itself radiant, silvered by the snow quilted
outside. They are tangled on the bed, and Cole is wonderstruck at
how he arrived here, how this unbreakable woman, this thorny
mountain gal, this wild rose, legitimized him, embraced him, and

she is marveling at the situation as well.

They lie there undone, snow sifting past the eaves. He had no expectation she would kiss him, they were saying goodnight and he looked lost, over his head, but trying to brave it, and maybe that's why she did it. She has always taken things in, abandoned things, stray dogs and cats, broken birds. Cole seems as singled out, but there is heart to him, he has guts, and a brain, and he's not bad on the eyes. His philosophy is off a few beats, how he expects he will breeze through Cope, this place on the margins, these people at the rim of the dark side. Because it is dire, make no mistake, it is ominous bad, what is bearing down, and he still expects he will make it, because listen to him now.

"I have an idea."

Rayann lies against her pillow, receives him with fortitude. "Figured you might."

"I want to call a meeting."

"With who?"

Cole leans up on his elbows. "With Wade."

"Oh my," Rayann says.

"Yeah," Cole says. "I thought it out. We can't drive out of here, you and me, Ty, John. They own the road."

"I never said I was goin, Cole."

"No, you didn't. Because we can't drive out of here."

Rayann raises off the pillow, frowning at him. "This gonna be one of those circular ideas comes back around on itself?"

He grows serious. "No. It's straightforward. I'm going to tell Wade I'm skiing off the backside of the mountain."

She takes this in.

"You're telling Wade your skiing off the backside."

"Yes."

"Why?"

"To get help."

"To get help."

"Yes."

She reels inwardly. He brings himself level with her. "I'm not leaving this mountain, he's not gonna know about it. So I just lay it out. I turn it into a contest."

"A contest."

"I challenge him."

Rayann decides Cole is disoriented, tries to ease it through.

"He won't like that."

"Not at all. He'll have to take me up on it."

"Uh huh. How's that gonna work out?"

Cole swings his legs off the bed, the window framing him. "I haven't ironed out the details yet. But it's a winner-loser deal. If I beat him to the finish line, I win."

She tests his sanity. "What do you win?"

"You."

He has her focus, even in the dark, and suddenly he's not so disoriented. He is intent. This time, she is not the rescuer. He thinks he will rescue her.

"You break my heart," she says.

"In a good way?"

"Can't make a deal with Wade. He'll go back on it."

"I know that. Listen. If I beat him down, I can get help. I can get the law up here."

She centers her eyes on him. "There won't be time for you to bring the law up."

"Hey," Cole says confidently, "I move fast. All downhill."

She wants to weep for him. "Into the hero snow goes you."

He says, "You got a topo map?"

"You haven't figured out how you're gettin down?"

"I'll find the fall line."

He grins. Rayann does not. The snow sifts past the window. They are left with that.

Chapter 30

The sun has not been seen for days, but Carla watches the vaulted sky darken and knows that day is declining behind the mountain. She has a single window in her station, her cube behind the Mayor's so-called office, her view is of the exterior stairs leading up, and past the stairs, the snowbound parking lot. There is only one vehicle down there, her own, a beat-up four-wheeler of Japanese origin and untold miles, an appliance, really, the cloth interior shredded and the ashtray overflowing.

She smokes too much, but gives thanks she is not a drinker, and that makes Jim Ainsworth hard to take sometimes, when he holes up, when he wraps himself around a bottle and it's a slow drag on the clock until he comes up for air. Carla suspects he's involved in that now, because she hasn't been able to pick him up, and no calls in, and it's time to shut down. She worries about him, because she likes him, though he would never suspect that, or probably even cast a thought her way. So she keeps her head down and they carry on a two-way exchange, a radio relationship, and share only their rueful knowledge of Cope's every wayward event.

Carla gathers her coat and purse. She'll have to cut the deputy loose for the night, and the hamlet will be without the both of them until morning. She's tucking the telecommunication center in bed – the Motorolas, two computer monitors, the keyboard, the headphones with mic. Priority Dispatch. Medical, Fire, Emergency Nurse, and Police, all funnel through here, the neural network of a one-unit hamlet. Count on hours, if not days, for what you might need. The Mayor is often out, but when she cuts costs, this is where the scissors close.

Turning out the lights, Carla catches a gaunt reflection in the window, a spector standing on the landing of the stairs. She freezes, making out a man she knows of.

Bob Gates. He has a fire-ax resting over his shoulder. He motions that she should open the door.

Carla obeys, and Gates boots in. He scans the meager

system that keeps Cope humming.

    She slips past Gates, and before heading down the stairs, she issues him a warning.

    "J.A. will hear about this."

    Gates doesn't even turn to her, speaking through his beard.

    "J.A. is radio silent."

*

It is dark, the kind of mountain dark that is tangible, a darkness that swims and surges, that physically occupies space. Cole Cantwell doesn't know where the wolfpack is, he just knows they are out there, so the meeting he calls takes place on the plateau outside the Zelda Mine. That frigid evening he takes the Jeep against Rayann's wishes and tracks up the mountain, following the switchbacks to the end of the road. There, he trespasses, builds a fire that will be seen across the valley. And he waits. He feels he has taken leave of his body, that he walks on air. A proper way to feel for the downslopes ahead, being on terms with the atmosphere.

    Cole stands for hours, the cold biting his backside, his front against the flames, the life-giving heat. He tosses rounds into the blaze when they are needed, the wood is plentiful and heaped nearby. He has brought no weapon, no form of self-defense, if it comes to that he wouldn't get off the plateau anyway. He makes out the heavens when the clouds glide apart and he feels minor, the plans of the earthbound, the infinitesimal, of no cosmic weight.

    It is deep into the night when they show up. Bob Gates has arrived at the edge of the fire with no visible assistance, he is just there, has been for a while, staring at Cole across the heat. A rifle is slung on one shoulder, an AK, and his garments are as stiff as his frozen beard.

    Cole searches for Gate's companion, finds Wade Deal in the dark behind Cole's own place at the fire. They have materialized like apparitions from opposing directions, insured there is no ambush, and Cole has never been more vulnerable in his bid to save the day. The quest feels especially wobbly, now that the two of them stand true and real. He wonders where the third man is.

Wade moves aside him, carrying a strong, unclean scent. His features are like hardwood, his gaze fixed. Cole sees no trace of clemency in that gaze, his own mortality mirrored there.

The man's voice cuts the heat. "You steal my rifle?"

Cole sinks inwardly, retains his footing.

"Can you steal something that's already stolen?"

Wade stares. Gates grouses.

"Dead man talk."

Wade Deal steps closer. He is like packed stone, immovable.

"That rifle is spoils. I'll reclaim it a little later."

His meaning settles over Cole.

"I have a proposal," Cole tells him.

Wade Deal and Bob Gates meet eyes. Cole is a stripling, a titmouse. Imagining a treaty. Wade's stare returns to him.

"Well?"

"Race down the mountain."

The black eyes snap at him.

"The backside," Cole says. "Winner hits the highway first."

Gates says across the fire, "What's he win?"

"He just keeps going."

"And the loser?" Wade asks.

"Loser stays here."

The blaze cracks. All three aim into it, Cole because he'd rather not contemplate either man's visage.

Wade says, "You'll lose. Legitimately, or because you threw the race to me. I'm down some funky road and you get Rayann free and clear?

Cole considers the statement. "I never thought of that."

Wade breaks no smile. "Like hell."

They assess each other.

"You estimating me?" Wade asks.

The flames pound, Cole can hear his own blood pound. He has taken leave of the foundation under him.

"Just trying to judge the angle."

"You'll be dead before that happens."

Cole is stabbed by Wade Deal's pupils.

Wade says, "What you got? Some high-tech lightweight snow-carvers that'll rocket you to first prize?"

"That would be the best scenario."

Wade studies him, seemingly in a new light.

"You ski the backside. I'll be along."

"Got it."

Wade moves out, Gates joining him. "You get past me," Wade says, "don't look back."

The dark takes them. And that could be the end of this phase, it could grant Cole a little more time, but instead he is guided by a hazardous, foolhardy impulse and he speaks out.

"Why do you do it?"

He hears them stop somewhere out there.

Hewn by shadow, Wade's features appear.

"Survival, flatlander. Of all the beasts in the wild, we are the foremost carnivores. We are that because we consume the centers of our enemies. We rule by fear."

The fire lights the prominences of his face, renders it almost transparent. Beneath the surface of his head, it is as if Cole can view his inner workings, the tireless gears that drive his derangement.

"Maneaters," Wade Deal says. "In the woods, the gorge, the mountaintop, fear reigns."

He recedes into the dark. "Tradition dies hard."

They are silent in going. The cold latches down.

Still, Cole stares after them.

Chapter 31

At first light, the mountain looms large. Macchus and Ida Deal bring out the mules, two jacks and a jenny, all good on steep snowy terrain and loose rock. Horses got crazy on the tight sections with the valley straight below, they had been known to take flight, where the mules are considered in their footing, and in their entire way of life.

The conditions aren't ideal for an excursion into the alpine, but they know a route up the west face where the snows are more manageable. The mules aren't shod. Macchus pulled the shoes, they ball up the snow in the hoof and hinder progress. Loaded into the trailer, they haul the animals to the terminus of a forest service road where they tack them up, the hinny with a packsaddle and pannier.

The day is gone by the time they've made the hard climb to their destination. They make camp in the dark, wind rattling through the dead limbs overhead. Macchus raises the tent, Ida strikes a fire in circled rocks.

"It's a given he knows we're here," she says.

Macchus adds, "Should he still survive."

"You plan to outlive him?" Ida asks.

His seamed eyes dwell on his loyal wife.

"With you as my rock, I-Deal. I know you'll still be standing when kingdom comes."

At daylight, a forgotten meadow opens into view. It had been a hardscrabble homestead when Macchus was a boy and there is not much of it left. No fencing remains, but the cramped cabin a few generations of Deals inhabited has not entirely sunk into the ground. Ida and Macchus peer into the shadowed, off-kilter doorway and sense emanations, tortured histories stirring. No one just passes through this place, it is difficult to reach and remote from anything useful or scenic. The trees are spiky, the earth leached. Ghosts drift, half-formed.

They seek a council with the Old Man, who might be using

the sunken cabin for shelter, or maybe he's sheltering in the deep of a ledge in the rock higher up. Macchus comes onto the cave while searching for some sign of the patriarch and spots what could be an exit cut for cookfire smoke. Or it could be this is where the old one keeps his armory dry, a 22. varmint plinker, and his main gun, a black powder muzzleloader older than he is. Macchus remembers that rifle, it could shoot a quarter-mile. The Old Man squeezed out every yard of it and was a dead shot.

He is elusive as smoke in the wind. He stopped going into town before the Deal's only son was born and his continued existence is no more than an anecdote. Periodically, in the darkest hours, an isolated wailing carries down from the pinnacles and his legend persists.

Macchus last set eyes on the Old Man a decade ago. Even then he was skeletal, hooded in deerskins stitched with sinew and living on what he wrenched from the mountainside. He was a piece of the mountainside, wore the same hues of stone and dirt and sap. He ate any and all mammal life, from bear to marmot, also brook trout, boiled roots, wild onion, pinyon, chokecherry, and the soft innards of birch and pine. In a channel downhill is a stream, free-flowing only a few months a year, otherwise under a staircase of ice, supplying water either way.

Taking the provisions at hand were skills the old man gave to Macchus, but they were not given generously, nor as a father to a son. Failure to watch closely, to not master the gutting of a heaving cavity with a few swift strokes, exacted punishment with closed fists. The old bastard was spare but fearsomely strong and Macchus' formative years of deep privation and brute labor were punctuated by collisions of bone on bone. Before he rolled up his few belongings and left the mountain for good, he was instructed in a final ceremony that case-hardened his soul. He contained that condition in everything he said or did thereafter, and that could have made him like the man who wrought him – unable to love. The son learned to surmount that fate – for the chosen few he bled love. His father's woman withered on the vine.

The Old Man was the keeper of a flame that brings no form

of light. He was the guardian of a ritual that honored endurance and perpetuity, the raw and binding deeds of the past. The imperative of existence became a ceremony, to be somberly transferred in lineage. Macchus met his obligation, anointed in blood. He handed down the unspeakable to his firstborn and Wade enacted not a rite of passage but a campaign of mayhem.

A lantern hisses, illuminates their camp. Ida Deal hauls her Dutch oven from the coals. Macchus rests on a stump. He watches the day burning out through the black bristle of the trees.

"It is coming to an end," he says.

"Consider it past due."

"The stalking, the killing, the bloody harvests."

She hands him a heaping plate, sits nearby.

"If the Old Man is not dead," he says, "decomposing under the snow, he knows this. He knows why we came."

Ida says, "The message won't veer him. Dead or alive, he will remain on the mountain."

Macchus speaks with conviction.

"And we will start down."

Chapter 32

John Ainsworth is grave watching his daughter leave. He has made
final adjustments to the V blade attached to the front of the
wrecker, a hydraulic lift that can stack snow higher than the roof.
He is glad Rayann knows her way around a shovel, pushing,
scooping, carrying, backdragging, and she never bangs the plow
up. But Cole is in the cab with her, his gear strapped to the deck,
and that means he is off on his mission and she is aiding him. He
watches them pull out, heading down Main Street.

Time is short and they are up against it. The young man's
approach of challenging Wade Deal to a contest in his own
backyard is pure folly, and Rayann will be left with nothing in the
end. She will lose her bright new lover and her father can only
offer his threadbare, dying embrace. She rates so much more, from
her dad, from life, but somehow she got saddled with just about
everything that can go wrong. He wanted to hug her tightly before
she left, he wanted his heart against hers, but he held back. She
didn't need his lack of faith on top of everything else.

*

They chain up the International before it starts to get slippery. Cole
has experience with chains, they each take a side and are done in
half the time. Toward midday, Rayann has shoved her way through
six miles of uphill drift, saving Cole hours in his quest to the steep
side of the mountain. The wipers can't keep up with the white
blizzard flying from the V blade as they scuff through snow knee-
deep and part it to either side.

On a section with good visibility she hands over a paper
bag with some weight in it. "Put it in your backpack."

"What's this?"

"Peanut butter and jelly sandwiches."

He is warmed by the gift. "That's domestic."

"Get hungry enough, you'll choke em down."

She slows, working the plow's joystick, running the wings

forward to match the grade.

"Dad managed to dodge them for years. Eight years old, it was my job to pack his lunch. I found half-eaten sandwiches all over the garage. Some of em qualified as relics."

"So you're not a deli person?"

"Nor a cook. My mother handed that down. Had no concept of what to do with a stove."

"But your mother was a beauty."

"How would you know?"

Rayann glances over, and Cole is enlivened. She is her usual orderly and foxy self.

"Look at the evidence," he says.

She works the plow. "Just a mountain gal. I told you that."

"And I ask you, what could be better? Pirouetting naked through the glades. Trailing songbirds and wildflowers. Fawns."

She absorbs that, withholding her laughter.

"Even you overstepped yourself on that one."

He does not watch their progress, he watches her.

"Because you make me light-headed."

"You gonna get serious about what's out front?"

"When the time comes."

"The time is at hand."

They are in the deep snow, banks at five feet, and what was roughly horizontal is now vertical dead ahead. Their path has ended, the slopes towering upward.

The truck comes to a stop. She parks the shifter, leaves it running, is out of her door before he can stop her. He kicks out of the wrecker and she is already on the deck unlashing his gear. She swings his backback over to him, his skis, boots, poles.

She jumps off the deck, he sets aside his equipment, studying the best route to the ridge.

"It's all business now," he says.

"Got a cattle trail winding up."

He glances at her. She stares upward. Then she faces him.

"You see that?"

"Yeah," he says, not seeing anything but her. "It looks like something I could skin my way up."

"Let's not drag this out," she says.

"You crying?"

She stares at him, her eyes obscured by her dark glasses. "Makes you think that?"

Cole's glove brushes her cheek. "Got a tear line here."

"Snow melt."

"I get it." He opens his pack, removes his rolled-up climbing skins. "Your dad's running out of time. Your son stands to get sucked in by Wade…"

He stands a ski up, begins smoothing the skin to the base. "Uncle J.A., as fucked up as he was, is gone…"

"Now I got to say farewell to you."

He peers over at her. "Look at you. Built to endure. Nothing can topple you. I'm coming back, Rayann."

She nods. She steps onto the running board under the door Cole exited. They hold a long gaze, a picture of each other that can be stored as a sacred memory.

"I love you, Cole Cantwell."

Then she slips inside the cab, shutting the door after her. The diesel engine clatters as she reverses the truck into a bank and pivots her way back onto the track down.

"That hurts," Cole says, to no one but himself, the wrecker steaming away. When the vehicle fades, he uprights a ski, begins applying his second skin, uttering what could pass for final words.

"It's all on you now."

Chapter 33

Up here at elevation it is a bluebird day, immaculate, cerulean, the cloudless vista across the lowlands sweeping all the way to the banded deserts of Nevada. It is a sporting day, a good day to die, as Cole phrases it, though he is not at all prepared to. Stay breathing is what's called for, breathing and in one piece. Something of a demand, now that he is confronted with the mountain's backside.

It looked feasible on the topo map Rayann came up with. Having prepared his skis for the downhill, balanced on the ridgeline, taking the sweep of the glacier in, maybe it is. The first maneuver is the cliff drop just below him, a sheer plunge before he can snap his weight onto the skis and gain control. Further downhill is a lunarscape of black rock convulsing up from the snow. It descends some distance and he needs to fit himself into the couloir that snakes between its jagged walls. That will be a tight chute, and after it flashes by who knows what he'll run into, because nothing further below is visible. The topo showed a myriad of potential obstacles down there but also some wide aprons where opportunities abound for straight-lining at max speed for a thousand yards.

The bigger worry is Wade Deal. Is he going to take a shot at him from the trees, or is he popping up downhill on snowcarvers of his own? Beneath the mountain man trappings, is he a formidable downhill sprinter? What about his associates, the bearded maniac, or the space-eyed giggler, who hasn't been seen lately. Whatever they have in store, they'll have to match mobility and acceleration. Cole makes a very rapid moving target.

The avalanche report is the snowpack is stable, and it looks it, no mush visible, just plush virgin snow. Blower snow. Powder heaven. Everything is first tracks up here, a black run of the highest order. Cole is gripped, confronting what's ahead.

Whether sport, or war, it's the same imperative. Claim the mountain. Stay upright. Survive.

He takes a footing, his skis crunching into the snow, wide

skis, with rocker and camber built for the steeps. Working his boards out over the rim, he gauges the course he will take when he hits the slope below the headwall. He has arrived here unmoored, not tethered to anything firm. He is operating on intuition, trusting his instincts. From here on, it's luck and terrain.

And he is off.

He skates out into the atmosphere, dropping past the face of the shining wall. Centered over his skis, he extends his legs as the slope below rushes up. He lofts onto it, his knees springs, and bent into the wind he takes his line, slicing down the backside.

He tightens the wide arcs he is turning as the rocky ledges ahead rear up. The entry into the couloir makes a rugged doorway, not much larger than his own width. He takes aim on it, gathering himself in and sheering through it.

The jutting rock walls blink past him, he tracks the floor winding through them, shifting constantly, threading a tight channel, avoiding the projections, keeping his arms attached to his torso. He questions if this chute has ever been skied before. Does it end at a freefall, or the deadly flank of a boulder?

It ends in neither. A bend comes up, whipping past it he sees the channel sweeping into the mouth of an ice cave under the snow. In an instant he is inside it, the path stony, low light infiltrating the roof. He ducks sharply as the roof squeezes down on him, the metal edges of his skis bleeding sparks. Skating the passage almost sideways, he scrapes through darkness for what seems a long time. The roof rises and light returns.

An exit appears, a wide tear in the snow, the sky out beyond. He is back over his legs as he shoots from the tube, launching into frosty air. A wind-carved cornice emerges below, not a good landing place, his skis skim it, chunking through the outer lip. A fracture line rips open, the surface softly caving in, and the cornice goes, nothing underneath the wave of snow.

Cole tucks lower and closer to his skis, intent on gaining even a small degree of speed, intent on dodging the tons of snow and ice sliding loose behind him. Touching down, he cuts into the slope, the snowslide on his heels, a wintery upheaval that in moments will bury him. He won't outrun it and his thoughts flash to survival, the beacon he carries, the signal lost to the wilderness, and no snow shovel to dig his way out.

Out of the slide an ice block crushes toward him, he hears it more than sees it, hears the size of it. To his right he sees a rise and pivots for it. It forms a ramp that kicks him airborne as the slide claims the place he occupied. He tightens forward into the jump, seeking something worthy to land on.

He hits firm snowpack, rotates to a stop, parked free of the tumbling terrain. He watches the slide pour into a trough, raising a heavy mist.

Now it's a traverse, with Cole carving horizontally across the slope. He's on the north face, it's staying powdery, and opening up ahead is an apron of unmarked whiteness. It heartens him. He has a wide field of visibility, a strong grade to maintain speed, nothing in his way until he hits the subalpine tree line, hazy and snowed under in the distance below.

*

It starts well, all the elements coming together, big rifts of powder bursting up, enveloping him in a shivering silver cloud. He has gained significant ground, the grade, gravity, hurling him forward.

A ledge not previously visible now materializes. In minutes he is skiing onto it, the ground below coming into view. Gouged out of the snow, a crevasse rips across the icefall.

Cole turns his skis into the mountain, sheeting snow skyward and halting at the brink of the ledge. He studies the chasm below, its depth, which he can't ascertain, and its width, which he can. Then he locks his eyes on a trail cutting toward the crevasse and ending at its very rim.

It is a sled trail. Snowmobile. The trail cuts off at the forward rim, and startingly, it continues on the far rim, chopping through a drift and vanishing. Reading the signs, the conclusion is the rider and the machine leapt the span.

Cole estimates it at twenty feet across, questions why the unstable edges at either side didn't give way. Did the rider know where solid snowpack was, where to leap and where to land? That would mean he had expert knowledge of this crevasse, and in terms of a race to be won or lost, he is now in the lead.

The crevasse opens and closes across the glacier. There is no time to search for a go-around. He'll have to make the same leap the snowmobile did. If Wade Deal can sling four or five hundred pounds of sled across, Cole can sling his skis across. He has a running jump from up here, the same jump the rider took.

He picks up the sled trail, finds a clear example of the treads the sled wears. They are high-altitude, with long lugs for the deeps of the mountain. Those longer lugs will cut down top speed, but if it comes to an all-out sprint for the finish line, Cole is unlikely to keep up. His advantage is lightness, agility, the ability to outmaneuver his opponent.

Following the sled trail to the edge of the crevasse, he reels at the depth of it. It plunges further than he can see, into deep blue shade, a solid argument for making sure there is enough momentum to complete the jump.

The plan is simple.

Back to the ledge. Build some steam. Lift off.

Cleave the atmosphere.

Touch down.

Chapter 34

The weightlessness is inspirational, soaring over the ravine that waits to swallow him. Below his skis, he has a prime visual of the inner crevasse, the playland turquoise light of it, the sparkling pillars of its walls, the lower reaches sectioned by shadows so dense they seem to have substance and volume. He can almost feel the chasm shift beneath him, hear its sonorous tones, the great mass of it cracking, splitting, ripping upward through the crust.

The opposite edge comes up, Cole's skis taking hold of the beaten snow where the sled landed, his weight coming down. The brittle shelf remains intact, bears him forward and away, the expanse of the lower glacier out before him once again.

It is a moderate descent here, a wide, sweeping run through gentle terrain. The midday sun bathes the slopes, warms his back. Thirsting and ravenous, he skids onto a flat place, plants his poles. He pours bottled water down his throat and goes through two of Rayann's sandwiches. The meal is primary but lifegiving and he thanks her and gives thanks also for his good fortune that in the uncertainty of his life he found her.

A pang shoots through his chest, that she could look through his guise, his dashing arrangement, the together man he pretended to be, and find someone to fall in love with. That he'd given his heart to her he did not question. Against the wilds he moves through, the absence of her leaves a cavity in him, he longs for her form and her spirit, and his day is far from done.

A dissonance comes to him, a dim disruption of the silence that enfolds the mountain. He scans the fringes of the glacier and sees movement. An object skims the snowpack.

It assumes shape.

A snowmobile, a rider, the rip of the two-stroke heard now, no terrain to dampen the noise, just unobstructed space, and no cover for Cole.

He slings his pack on, grips the poles. He'd been thinking with favorable ground and more good luck he could make the highway before nightfall. But the inevitable is closing in.

The sled, now front-wise to his view, whines across the powder. The rider is determined, standing over his seat.

*

The sub-alpine tree line below Cole is obtainable, a matter of a few thousand feet, if he can gain enough speed to stay ahead, a task he needs to pursue immediately. Once in the trees, he'll find the tightest line and finesse a course the sled can't fit through. Maybe he can leave Wade Deal up against a tree.

He shoves away, the grade dropping, Cole dropping with it, touching down, bent forward, straight-lining over the glacier. He is making good speed, but when he looks to his left the snowmobile has closed in, now only a few hundred yards out.

His hood edged with ice, Cole urges his skis on, tracking toward the stands of snowy conifers. The screaming sled bounces closer and he takes in the threat.

Spraying a white fantail, Wade Deal veers toward him, the stink of scorched oil staining the air. He is clad in thick brown furs, his head encased in stitched deer suede, a sort of winter mask. His black machine smokes, battered by years of forging trails where none exist. There is something bail-wired to the front of the cowl.

It is a skull. Cole's focus is on getting to the trees, he has no time to dwell on what rides the nose of the sled, but his suspicion as his insides shrink is that the skull is human.

Wade Deal singles Cole out, his pupils pinned through the holes of his mask.

He powers ahead of Cole, edging toward his line, he is trying to cut him off. As the snow-laden trees rush up, Cole blades his skis in, slowing enough for the sled to cross his path, then he carves left, accelerating into a stand of white pine.

He whips through the boughs of the trees, the space between them not as tight as he hoped, because he can hear the sled changing course, finding his tracks. Cole zigzags, dodging the pines, dodging the wells beneath them, the soft inescapable snow hollowed around the trunks. Sinking into a well, he would not climb out.

The two-stroke behind him gains volume. The ground slants steeply, rocks jutting, scraping his skis. Now dead in his path, the boughs of a fallen tree. He springs upward, his poles striking sluff loose from the branches as he clears them. Then he is back on the grade, whipping through the heavily wooded light.

He can hear the sled no more, and that may bode well. It is possible that Wade Deal lost his sled in the trees, hit a tree well, or stacked it up trying to thread the trunks. It is possible he flew into a trunk himself, and may his parts be scattered throughout the pines. The outcome could be tilted in Cole's favor, deliverance dawning.

Coming out of the trees, hitting a ramp of snowy rock, going aerial, those possibilities evaporate. The black sled is also aerial and it is now alongside him, its engine snarling in his ears. He never heard the man coming, his approach diffused by the trees, by Cole's pounding hopes for an end to him.

They pitch toward the rim of a headwall.

They drop over it.

Both align their angles. Both come down on the slope below in unison.

They are running parallel, only yards apart, scraping over ice and glare, bounding through drifts. If it were not fatal, it would be majestic, a pair of experts on their honed equipment, coordinating turns, slicing opposing arcs, soaring at the same time, skimming cornices, outcrops, troughs. The glacier before them is a falling sea of white, its crystalline surface thrown skyward by their skis and glinting in the sun.

When they get into the deep, Cole hopes for a break. His skis keep him surfaced, Wade Deal's snowmobile is starting to bog. He dismounts to unweight it, running alongside, his hands braced on the horns of the handlebars. As Cole leaves the snowfield, the other man swings back onto the sled.

He swiftly rejoins Cole. His two-stroke saws the afternoon to splinters and he is close by – bear hides, leathery mask, a gargoyle astride machinery shrieking at ten-thousand rpms. Cole gathers himself for the cliff edge he sees sliding toward him, its height, the terrain below, unknown.

The sled's skis, Cole's skis, are in one instant abreast and then he is in the wind and the sled is not. The rider has heaved his machine away from the rim, watching Cole meet the air, plummet.

That is Cole's last glimpse of him, and he knows he's been led into a non-recoverable drop. Airborne, the distance to the base is daunting. He has to come down right, no flopping ragdoll, ending in an explosion of limbs and strewn gear. He has the cliff's measure, he is angled properly with the face he falls along, he is positioned. The snowpack that rushes toward him looks like it might hold up.

He touches down, harnessing gravity, glides to firm ground. He seeks the line he can convert to an unobstructed run. He thinks he sees that line, the course he can take off the icefall, a way home.

A rocky chute awaits him, beyond it the slope is broad and unhindered. The ragged rider and machine are left behind and the sun is still high enough to light the final push to the highway.

The powder deepens.

He slides onto the snow bridge before he recognizes it, just a dark slit that his skis cross. He understands then that the crevasse beneath is almost entirely hidden, and with that the shelf under his feet, the icy covering delicately suspended, comes down.

He yells out as he crashes through the crust. He is upright at first, scraping his skis along the walls, shearing ice, trying to slow the fall. He bangs into an icy projection that collapses as it flips him, a jagged slot of sky flashing, the walls again, closing the sky off. He plunges on into the fissure.

His fall is arrested, jarred to a rib-cracking stop, the cold sting of loose snow sliding over him. He doesn't know how far he has fallen, or what he landed on, or what damage he has sustained. He doesn't even know whether he is conscious or knocked senseless. With any luck, he is dreaming, has dreamt the entire backside of the mountain, dreamt this abyss. With luck, the fix he has gotten himself into is only a bad dream he will wake from.

Or maybe, this time, he is dead to the world.

*

Leaning over his handlebars, studying the freshly opened fracture in the crevasse below, knowing how deep the chasm goes, Wade Deal feels some accord is due his vanquished enemy. He fought well, but he went the way of all challengers.

There is a hole in the deer suede for his mouth. It reveals a grim set of jaw, almost a grin. He contemplates the abyss in the mountain below and pronounces an epitaph, words spoken before, that in their bleakness comfort him.

"That's the beauty of it. You hear nothing."

Chapter 35

In Cope, an emergency meeting is called. Historically, few such meetings have taken place, but the Pastor is quick to offer his church and it serves ably as the venue. He stokes the parlor stove as agitated citizens file in and he has never witnessed such a level of attendance. The pews are filled back to the entrance. From the pulpit he looks them over, all the people who have never shown up for services but are quick to call him in for last rites to an ailing relative.

The Pastor picks out Rayann Ainsworth with her son Ty. Rayann is not a committed churchgoer, but she does make his eyes feel good and he allows her some leeway. He knows everyone out there, at least in passing, and he fronts them bravely, but for most, they are far from brothers or sisters. John Ainsworth, in attendance with his daughter and his grandson, is in that category, along with Quincy, the eternally silent black man with the yellow eyes, and he doesn't much like Althea's big-butted bossiness, or her kitchen man Juan with his sullen ways and his teardrop tattoo that indicates a term in prison. Hanson, the owner of the Cope Market, is no acolyte, a baggy-eyed lecher who fondles employees in the storeroom, and speaking of that, his cashier is very disagreeable, always coldly watching the Pastor count his change at the checkstand. There sits Carla, the radio woman, who reeks of cigarettes and can't locate a man, and how about this unshaven guy who has the temerity to attend the meeting in his bathrobe? In fact, the Pastor seems to recall, that is his name – Guy.

Probably, the person the Pastor has the least liking for is the Mayor of Cope, Patty Mandragon, a scary name and a scarier elected official. A chronic no-show, she exists under layers of red lipstick and blue eyeshadow, her face at once hot and cold, but otherwise makes no pretense to fashion. Today she wears a flannel shirt under sturdy overalls and waterproof boots. Making decrees agreed on by a city council of two, she is burly in her ways, and as far as the Pastor can see, has no morals or empathy. He reflects on this as he introduces her now.

"Folks, we have a difficult situation looming and that's why we're here. The Mayor wants to address our predicament, as best she can. Patty…"

The Mayor turns the pulpit into her podium, subtly bulling the Pastor out of her way. She blinks out over the room, her lashes thickly tarred.

"Pay attention, folks, because this is what I'm telling you: As of right now, Cope has no operational way to communicate with outside authorities. No radio dispatch, no wi-fi, no landlines. Quite frankly, we are up against it."

She oversees the unsettled reaction from the pews.

"Well, where in hell is our deputy marshal?" Guy, the man in the bathrobe is asking that question. "Where is mister strong-arm-of-the-law when he is most needed?"

The room stirs, comments made, the most alarming comment quieting the turnout.

"You don't want to know."

The Mayor fixes on the voice, her eyeballs encircled with tide-pool shadow. "Our radio operator said that. Carla, do you want to share your information?"

Heads turn to Carla, who steadfastly reports the situation.

"The dispatch center is in pieces. Bob Gates hacked it up. And looks like Wade Deal took out some utility lines. Gates said Deputy Ainsworth is radio silent."

"He's dead?" someone shouts. "Or his radio don't work?"

The question is drowned out by a general uproar. The Mayor bounces on her rubber-soled boots, waving her arms for order. "Okay! Okay! Tone it down! We have a deranged kill-pack holding this town hostage…"

Those in the pews resume silence.

"That's what I call them," the Mayor continues, "a kill-pack. They are out there, and they are coming in. We have to rally. We have to incorporate a defense. How many out there have firearms?

A forest of arms spear the air.

The Mayor nods. "I knew that, and I move that we set up a crossfire on Main Street."

A sheep rancher, ex-vet, has a question. "And what if that's not the point of entry?"

The Mayor scrutinizes him. "Are you some kind of military tactician? Of course it's their point of entry. There is no other entry. They roll in and we drill em."

"I don't know if you're familiar with their vehicle," Hanson, the Market owner says. "It's goddamn three-foot off the tires. Drive over anything. They don't need a road."

"You think about the crossfire?" the sheep rancher adds. "You're gonna have citizens murdering each other from each side of the street."

"Plus," Carla says, "Is that even legal? Shooting them down in cold blood? Without a statute?"

An unfamiliar voice wells out, a strong bass timbre.

"We are a stand-your-ground state."

It is Quincy, seated at the aisle, and his voice is unfamiliar because no one has ever heard him speak.

"Deadly force," he instructs, "would not likely result in a conviction if there exists imminent danger of great bodily harm."

For a moment, the proceedings halt, baffled stares directed the black man's way. The Pastor is most baffled of all. Why didn't Quincy express himself so cogently on the scriptures? Why didn't he give the least indication he could express himself at all?

"Maybe they don't really mean us harm," the Cope Market cashier suggests. "Maybe they're just prankin. Boys being boys."

Althea shudders. "These are not boys. Like the Mayor says, they're killers. I for one don't intend to have my throat cut in bed."

Ty Deal stands from his seat next to his mother. Rankled, he reminds everyone who he is.

"This is my dad you're talkin about."

Hanson tries to console him. "That ain't your fault, sonny."

Ty turns on him. "I'm proud of my dad. He's out there doin what it takes to survive. You can't even lift a box of potatoes. You got your stockgirls doin it when you don't have a hand up their dress and if you say another fuckin word about Wade I'll put a broadhead arrow in your ass."

The room dissembles, those gathered angered, affronted, in the commotion Hanson sneers. "Chip off the old block," and Rayann is on her feet, grabbing her son by the arm.

"You watch your mouth, Hanson"

Turning to Ty, she says, "And you just screwed yourself. We don't speak to others like barbarians. You lock your insolent butt in your room until I can deal with you."

Ty breaks free of her, stalks down the aisle. John Ainsworth, who has held his tongue, rises from his seat. He waits until the furor fades and he has the room's attention.

"You good people take your measures," he says. "I have a line on mine, and it will go straight to the heart of it. Main Street, off-road, don't matter which way they come in. When they appear, I will make them disappear."

Ty Deal, pausing at the exit, seethes, marking those words.

The Mayor has had enough. With no further ceremony, she vacates the pulpit, stonily making her way out. There is no plan for the citizenry, no safety net in place, and the Pastor is left with the shambles of the meeting. He stares out over the rows of anxious faces, the mutterings of discontent, and a haggard woman, one of his flock, asks for words of solace, hope.

"Is there a message, Pastor? Guidance from the Lord?"

The Pastor's glasses incline toward the rafters. He searches the cobwebs strung there, intent on detecting a Godly cadence from the skies beyond, something harmonic, comforting.

And finally, he has the answer.

"I'm sorry. I hear nothing."

*

They walk through the alleyway behind the gas station. Rayann is trying to forestall what is already crumbling, her father dead-set on his final engagement.

"They won't sneak their way in. They'll come right down the center of Main street."

"I know what you're thinking. Don't go near it."

John Ainsworth does not hear her.

"Cole will bring help, Dad. He's probably cleared the back of the mountain by now."

Her father turns to her. "False prospects, baby girl. But I will say this – it's always good to have a back-up plan."

Rayann stares bleakly ahead. "Custer thought he had one."

Chapter 36

The mountain coyote is traveling solo. His pack has been scattered across the alpine, trappers on their heels, their pelts scavenged for trim on fur collars. This one hasn't eaten for five days. His winter coat is tawny, etched with black and silver, dense with bristly guard hair and lush with underfur. He moves over the glacier with his large ears cocked and his nose down. He is starving, and also soundless, seeking movement under the snow. He searches for a weasel's tunnel, a vole's nest, the bite of blood, bone, organs, that will keep him alive for another night.

The coyote's attention swings toward a disruption, a cave-in at the edges of a fracture in the drift. He treads toward it cautiously, breathing in the scent of man, the elements of that world. At the rim of the break in the snow, the coyote sets his eyes on the deep below and smells hazard.

He crouches, lightly springs across the chasm of the fracture and soon he is gone. On the face of the mountain, he leaves behind only close-quartered tracks, imprints that dwindle toward the floor of the valley below.

*

Cole sees the movement. He doesn't hear the animal, just glimpses a fleeting blur, a furred shadow. He has pinned himself into a space between the crevasse walls, his ski boots jammed against one side, his back against the other. His feet are lower than his trunk and that has allowed him to struggle his way upward.

The crevasse is narrow here and appears to remain so all the way to the top. The going is slow. He plants one boot, braces his weight against that leg, plants the other boot above it, repeats the process. He estimates he is halfway up. It is slippery, frigid, he has to rest in position frequently, but as far as he can tell, he has sustained no major injuries in the fall. At the rim above priceless daylight is filtering away.

He wears the backpack, it has stayed with him and provides

padding for his back as he walks his way upward. His skis and his poles are lost. All were torn free. From the ledge he ended up on, his gear continued down into the blackness. If he makes his way out of these freezing walls, the rest of the journey will entail post-holing through the mountain snow in his ski boots. His leather boots are in his backpack, protecting him from shredding his back, but they would quickly freeze solid in knee-deep powder, as would his feet.

His breath steams, his lungs working hard. He is dismayed at how stunningly alone he is, how tremendously disadvantaged, but the burning inside him, the purpose that brought him to this juncture, remains. He has the strength and fortitude of his unbroken years, the cool-headed nerve of young men. His progress may be compromised but he has reserves of endurance, of will.

He expects to live, and thus he will.

It is apparent he will be spending the night on the mountain, and he deems it survivable. He is at tree level and once out will find enough downed wood to start a blaze that will hold the cold at bay, that will keep him alive through the sub-zero blackness closed like a tomb around him. At first light he will begin the descent to valley.

The sky over the crevasse has faded to the color of ash. His legs are shaking, boots braced. If he loses his grip it's back down to the ledge in a hurry, or off the ledge and into the abyss. There would be no coming back from either place, so the final twenty-feet to the rim is mandatory. What powers him, what keeps his blood on a burn, is the obligation to avenge himself. Wade Deal put him here. And Deal will now run riot in Cope. It is his for the taking. John Ainsworth will not stop him. Rayann will be singled out. She will not go down meekly.

Cole heaves his weight into his left leg, withdraws his right leg, and raising it, slams that boot higher into the wall. His thirst is savage and from his throat animal noises throb. He wants to scream in terror and rage but it would expend the last of his energy and he would never make the rim.

Which, if he is not deluded, is getting closer.

Chapter 37

Linus drives an LPG tanker and his route covers deliveries across the eastern Sierra. He travels endless highways, winding country lanes, narrow mountain loops, obscure alleyways, and one rutted trail that leads to a communal living situation he thinks isn't all that wholesome. The Propane Man is what they call him. He has a Christian name like any other man, but Linus never sticks in anyone's mind, it is easier to associate him with what he delivers.

It is a widely scattered territory, about as far-flung as they come. His time behind the wheel is solitary but he doesn't have much in the way of adversity. He is a bachelor, confirmed, and he has taken steps to regulate his life. No booze, number one, that party is over, he'd opened his doorway and Jesus walked in. Up with sun, pre-inspect the equipment, focus on the work. Manage the reels and hoses, the valves, the cylinders. Manage the customers. Smile and nod. Refer complaints to someone higher up and move on.

He'd pulled out of the pumping station at 5 a.m. with 2600 gallons of liquified petroleum gas, now it's late afternoon and all he has left is enough for his last call. With the wildfires and the power outages, demand is sky-high and it's tricky keeping up. But he handles it. He is invaluable, so management says, he knows his way around. Steady, deliberate, patient. Even so, snarls are unavoidable, and here comes one now.

Through the windshield, a straggler at the roadside. It is icy out there, the fields blanketed and his tanker truck slipping around some. He tracks the tire grooves in the sheeted surfaces, mastering the truck's high center of gravity, and he's always stayed upright. Now he has to touch the brakes because the man ahead has turned to him and is waving his arm.

It is policy not to pick up hitchhikers, but this one is more than that. As the truck closes in Linus can see the man is in trouble. He is hooded, his face dark with grime, he looks to be in his twenties. His gloves are black with mud, his cold weather garments wet and torn. A limp pack is strapped to his back, the leather boots on his feet are encased in ice.

The truck comes to a stop. On Linus' part, there are long moments of cataloging – homeless, mentally ill, killer on the loose? The man stares up through the window, reading Linus, and he nods, holding his gloved hands wide open.

"I need the police," he shouts.

It could still be a ruse, but the Propane Man has a back-up piece within reach, a common sense measure for safety rather than sorrow. On the other hand, it doesn't look like the dude's got much future out there, if in fact, he lasts out the day.

Linus motions the young man inside and Cole Cantwell steps up, swings the opposite door open, clambers into the warming cabin. He is shaking with the cold, he is an odiferous and foreign presence, and he recognizes that.

"Thanks," he says, wanting to put things at ease. "I was up on the mountain all night. Hit a crevasse, lost my skis. It was a hike coming down. I'm Cole, by the way."

The driver makes a quick examination, starts the tanker truck forward. "Linus. The Propane Man. You say this is a police matter?"

"Yeah."

"We got any bad guys hereabouts?"

"Not hereabouts."

You spent the night up there with no shelter?"

"I made a big fire."

"How's your feet? That don't look ideal."

"It's not. But I can still feel something attached to the end of my legs."

The truck bangs and rocks over the frost and Cole takes his bearings. The road they are on is a single lane running below the foothills he worked his way down from. It narrows into the misty landscape ahead.

"I was shooting for Three-Ninety-Five," he tells the driver.

"That's a few miles east. You say this is a police matter?"

"Right. I'm looking for the nearest sheriff's station."

Linus glances at him. "Nearest is thirty-miles south. I made a delivery there this very morning, and I can tell you ain't no officers free. They're all out evacuating folks ahead of the Bristlecone Fire."

Cole takes that in, failure looming.

"You got an emergency?" Linus asks.

Cole nods ruefully. "Pretty much."

Linus squints ahead, into a possible solution.

"There *is* a substation."

Cole is quick to find out more. "We anywhere near it?"

"Not too far. It's up the mountain."

Up the mountain isn't the direction Cole is looking for. "I'm trying to pinpoint where exactly."

"Place called Cope."

Cole is silent, trying to salvage the animation for a response.

"Cope," he finally says.

Linus grins, happy to be the bringer of good news.

"You're in luck. Cope's my last delivery."

The tanker crushes forward and within Cole hope collapses. He manages a nod. Not in affirmation. In acknowledgement that all progress forward leaves a path to its beginning, and that is the path that carries him on.

Chapter 38

While Bob Gates waits for Wade to return, he works on fortifying the quad-cab for their raid into Cope. They had discussed bolting on steel panels with gun slits to shield the pickup's windows, with some type of barrier preventing the tires from being shot out. "Nah," Wade decided, "They hit the tires, truck will still roll. Take some time to go flat, and we will have reached our objective by then." Instead, they concentrated on armor for the windshield, side glass and doors.

Bob Gates is a welder but obtaining material takes some effort. The gas station is an obvious donor but John Ainsworth is patrolling it vigilantly, deer rifle in hand. Gates doesn't have time for a pitched firefight that might go one way or the other, so he looks elsewhere and finds what he needs in the junkpile at the end wall of the box canyon.

There is plenty of automotive sheet metal available, but bullets punch right through the light-gauge panels. When he walks over a stack of rusty plates in the weeds, he has his resource. Ferrous stuff, alloy of iron, cast-iron itself. He breaks out the quad-cab's windshield, preps the gas welding set-up in the pickup bed, and spends a day in the canyon. Gate fabricates rough shields out of the plates, burning slots through his chosen window armor with the plasma cutter, clamping the plates into position on the exterior door and window frames, welding them in place with perfect stringer beads. In a burst of inspiration he salvages a woodstove door and fixes it in place ahead of the driver. The thick ceramic glass fixed in the iron serves as a viewing port and he thinks it a nice touch.

Gates is a golden arm with a torch. With the fizzle dancing against his face shield, he constructs a vehicle of purpose and annihilation, creating a supremely sick and monstrous machine. He stands and admires in the last of the daylight.

Wait until Wade eyeballs this.

*

The gas station garage gets cold at night, and John Ainsworth is more or less camping out in it. He has arranged his bag at the wall heater in the office and he only eats once a day, a meal that Althea brings across the street from the café. The café is closed to the public at this point, but John sees her in there fussing around. She can't separate herself from the warm, breathing depot that fed the inhabitants of Cope, that completed their well-being, gave them friends and conversation. The café centered folks, enlivened their souls, if they had a soul to begin with, and John knows a few who were born without one.

That is Althea's mission, to provide, to nourish, to foster kinship, and locking the door left her without purpose. So John's meals are grand plates, though the best he can do is pick at them and they are still heavy with food when she comes to collect. She never says a reproving word about the waste, they pass pleasantries that overlook the coming siege and then Althea humps back across the street with her bus tray.

John knows his appearance is worrisome. The cancer has flung itself to distant organs, his bones show, his tone is green-gray, his strength has emptied. He can work the bolt on his 30-30 okay, but anything unduly physical is a tall order. He *wants* them to come in, he can't hold out much longer, and it is important to give them a fitting goodbye.

The streets outside are under a warm front. All is slush and traces of the coming spring are in the air. Rayann boots her way through soft ground to visit her father daily. There is not much to discuss because he has made up his mind – and that is decisively that – but there is still much to convey. They do that in silence, holding one another, and these are the only instances where John allows tears to flow. He hates people crying about what can't be changed, and it is especially hard on him when those tears are spilled by his one and only daughter, who has so many other reasons to weep but never does.

They are a blood union, two forms silhouetted as one against the light in the glass of the garage door.

With her son's help, Rayann has rifled her father's stock of lumber and screwed boards to the inside windows of the bungalow, all fifteen of them, attic and main floor. She has also reinforced the entries, front and back, with steel straps fastened to the doorframes so the deadbolts can't be kicked through. Her current project is drilling gun ports in the window boards with a hole saw. Her father left her with an old shotgun but she found something better under her bed, a magnificent rifle of blue steel and polished walnut with a telescopic scope. This surprised her because it could only have been put there by Cole, who has never mentioned it, and also surprising was the considerable collection of dust and hairballs, indicating the length of time she had not cleaned under her own bed. In other circumstances, it would be an embarrassment, but priorities now hinged on more primal needs.

The house is dim with the windows sealed. Rayann and Ty exist there in a kind of tense gray dream. The consequences of the impending onslaught will be hard to accept and mother and son have different viewpoints on its outcome. Rayann sits Ty down at the kitchen table so they can arrive at an understanding.

"Wade is out of control," she says. "He has snapped. What was already horrendous is now a situation of life or death. You know he's coming in with the worst of intentions. My position on this is that we will aggressively defend ourselves."

She waits for her son's reaction. His gaze is sullen. She takes in his bristly hair, his dirty clothes, unchanged for a week. He is already removing himself from her, defying her household. When he speaks, his tone is stringent.

"My father," he tells her, "will destroy anything in his way to get what he is after."

Rayann is startled by his declaration. It sickens her, how her own child has cold-bloodedly summed up their respective positions.

"And what is that?" she asks, biting back despair. "What is he after?"

Ty's eyes blaze. "He's after me."

They hold a stare across the table. The heart of the matter has been spoken. Wade Deal is out to claim his begotten. The time has arrived for his son's rebirth, his transition into manhood. It will be a bloody rite of passage, nothing anchored will stand afterward. Ty will don animal skins, live as part of the pack. Barking. Ravaging. He says as much.

"The wild days are coming, mother."

Her anguish is a quiet shiver. There is no stopping him with reason or logic, no locking him in the basement. He will go where he is drawn. "Let's hear it," she says. "What else is on your mind?"

"I'm Wade's right hand man," he tells her. "Only thing I'll ask him is that you are spared. Your nagging, that sharp tongue, I'll be glad to leave behind, but you borned me, made a home for me, and we owe you somethin for that."

A wave of dread rises in Rayann.

"We," she says. "So it's already the two of you."

"We will run the mountain," Ty says, his gaze fixed not on her but on what lies ahead. "You'll hear us howling at midnight, the hours when you couldn't be more alone, and you'll know we are the rulers of our kingdom."

The boy stands from table. She is still, injured, grieving for all that's being lost.

"Anything else?" he asks.

"Yes," Rayann says, collecting her strength.

Ty huffs, lacking patience.

"That rifle I acquired," she says. "It has three rounds in the magazine and one in the chamber, it is scoped, and when Wade Deal appears in the crosshairs he will receive a magnum load."

The boy's features tighten, his eyes screwed on her.

"You really think you'll get off a shot?"

Her own gaze is firm, unyielding.

"A shot straight and true, sent with all my heart."

Chapter 39

Wade Deal credits himself with perception beyond normal human range, and he perceives Rayann's intent almost as she speaks it in the confines of her home. He will not make of himself her target, the girl can shoot, he will deal with her on his own terms.

In the meantime, Bob Gates has turned the quad-cab into a battle wagon, so they aren't entering Cope that morning in stealth mode, but it does not really matter now. The inhabitants are not going anywhere, they will quake inside their hovels, pray for invisibility, and because Wade is pressed for time, most will see the misery of a new day. He must be selective in who he dispatches, and it seems that a visit to the holy man, the puppet for the pious and the righteous, is the first order of business.

"This pickup is a heavy bastard," Wade says, once behind the wheel. The truck grinds and clanks and the view out the glass in the woodstove door has no peripheral. With the slabs surrounding them it is like riding in the turret of a tank. The whole arrangement looks on the wacky side, but Gates is proud of it, so no reason to step on his cake. It should protect against the stray bullet.

Not a hundred feet ahead, it does just that, the round banging against the metal and whining away. They are passing the Cope Market and Wade is pretty sure the shot came from that shithead Hanson, the owner, who is stationed somewhere on the premises.

"You clock that?" Gates says, beaming. "That half-inch plate sent that lead tail twixt legs."

"You done good, Bobby," Wade says, braking the pickup. It heaves to a stop and Gates runs the barrel of his AR-15 through the gunport at his side, tracks his laser scope across the building.

"No see him," he says.

"Could be on the roof," Wade suggests.

Gates inclines his weapon, squinting into the scope. He shifts his aim and says, "There he is. The roof. I got the red dot on his bald fuckin cranium."

Wade Deal leans in, eyes keen. "Well, talk to him."

Gate's rifle jumps, a quick burst hammering. He studies the results. "He's down."

"For the count?"

"Far as I can tell. How about I take out them big storefront windows on the first floor?"

Wade effects half a smile, indulging him. "We got a full day. Do it on a roll." He prods the battle truck ahead and Gates empties his magazine through the gunport, the rounds cracking, glass heard cascading to the street.

"Insurance cover that?" he asks.

They grind on.

The church is dark and desolate, the weather unsettled. The wind of an oncoming storm gusts, and they witness the cross tilted over the porch lose its battle to stay upright and flatten to the roof.

"God didn't do it," Wade says.

The atmosphere inside is spectral, the resident ghost found kneeling in prayer before the altar. He hears them walk in. The wind comes in with them, skidding the discarded handout of a psalm across the planks. The Pastor is robed, his eyes are closed to better focus his communication with the Creator. His voice is strong today, stronger than he has heard it in a long time.

"No weapon that is fashioned against you shall succeed, and you shall confute every tongue that rises against you in judgment…"

They stand behind him, figures of gloom.

Wade Deal grips the strap of the black rifle looped over his shoulder, stares down on the Pastor, whose words resound.

"This is the heritage of the servants of the Lord and their vindication from me, declares the Lord."

"Turnin into a sermon," Gates says.

Deal issues a warning. "Hold that God talk, preacher."

The Pastor's eyelids open, his pupils fevered. He seeks the courage to continue and finds it.

"Behold, I have given you authority to tread on serpents –"

Wade Deal seizes the rear of the Pastor's collar and hauls him backward off his knees. Gates makes way as he is dragged on his back along the center isle.

"Serpents and scorpions," the Pastor cries, *"and over all the power of the enemy..."*

His weight in Deal's grip is insignificant, his robes sweeping the floorboards. The intruder pulls him to the church's entrance.

"... and nothing shall hurt you," the Pastor concludes, and he is through the doorway, sliding across the porch, bumping down the steps, and left on his back in the waste of the yard, Wade Deal rising over him.

"This is your authority," Deal says. "The mud and the slush. You got no house of worship." He leans down, his fractured features taut. "There *is* nothing to worship."

The Pastor stares steadily up at Wade, wind cutting the yard. Gates leans at the porch rail, beard split by a grin.

He has transcended fear. God has at last come into him. God has shored his heart, his spirit, his soul. He rises to a sitting position.

"Mud. Slush. God's house is where I serve him."

Wade motions to Gates, who starts for the armor clad truck.

"Then you'll be at home, preacher. With rocks for your bed. Living in your rags. Shitting in the weeds. The winds, the lightning, the fire of the sun, will flay you."

The Pastor regards him, unswerving. Gates reappears with a gas can and boots his way up the porch steps.

Wade Deal, the beast in man's form, poses a question. "Ever eat maggots, pastor? When the hunger claws, you will. Squatting in a lean-to, unrecognizable. Least of all to yourself."

He leaves the Pastor, following Gates into the church.

"Life in God's fields ain't kind."

Chapter 40

Inky smoke piles across the afternoon – carbon monoxide, carbon dioxide, hydrogen cyanide gas. Soot black as tar. The toxicity stings John Ainsworth's eyes, he is seated in the wrecker a few blocks away, and without actually seeing the blaze knows what it consumes. Scraps of dark paper whirl, the wind thermal, laden with the formaldehyde of burning furniture. So go the scriptures and the pews. The altar, the cross. Jesus, naked and agonized, nailed to it.

Gunfire thuds and pops, rapid concussions decimating the foundations of Main Street. John's fists clench the steering wheel, his hatred for them surging, caught in his throat. His 30-30 rests buttstock foremost between the front seats. It is a Winchester, a lever-action implement of the West, a storied deer slayer, or anyone other that deserves wearing a target. The rifle is there for back-up. John has larger defensive measures in mind.

From his position, the view is limited, a hundred feet or so of the road ahead. A flurry comes down, crystals beading the glass. His International is in the trees, their trunks and boughs screening it, diesel engine clicking at a steady idle. The gunfire has ceased and John expects an appearance will shortly be made, that their path of destruction will take them finally this way. The nose of the wrecker is girded, the v-blade formed in an iron wedge, but not parting snow this time. It constitutes a lot of tonnage, the plow, the truck, speed gathered, hurtling forward.

John's thoughts fly as he waits. He is in his seventh decade on this earth, and half of that gone, but it is still too early to depart his existence. So many loose ends remain, things he will never have a chance to tie down, the greatest among them his daughter's fortunes. The gas station is a lease, and the inventory financed must be paid off. She will have his savings account, what he scraped together over the years, and that will retain her, at least until the next misfortune comes her way.

He has led a life of few regrets, but now, at the end of it, he holds bitter disappointment, that he failed to protect Rayann from what the world would hand her. Wade Deal spoiled everything he came in contact with. Even his son is tainted. And now the daughter will once again bear the burden of attending to the father, his final dispersal, what is brokenly left of him.

There is no other way. What he leaves her with is necessary in order to save her. He can do that much, remove the fangs from her heart, the contagion from her soul. Remove Wade Deal from the world he infects.

Too little, too late, as far as brother Jim goes. Was there ever any chance of saving him to begin with? An authentically tragic figure, John was sworn to him, but it was work, pulling him out of his bad decisions, and in these last years he was too far buried for rescue. J.R. was unlucky, in war, in life, in love, he wore that on his back, and it was mostly self-inflicted.

John's brother was convinced he had the code to how things really worked, and when the code failed, time and again, he became even more determined to apply it. John's counsel to him, his place as his guardian, lost its effect. He watched Jim sink his marriage, estrange his kin, alienate the public he served, and retreat into the dingy cell of his being. Althea has talked about the last day she saw J.R, how he told her he had a meeting, that he was heading to route 395. He seemed uplifted, she said, and before he walked out he gave her his smile, the one that dissolved fears and doubts. John thanked God that in Jim's final hours he found something to fasten onto, that he called on his misplaced bravery, harnessed it, used it to defy what descended on him that day.

There is already talk of sightings, of a location on the steep flanks of the canyon where Jim Ainsworth's crumpled truck has come to rest. It would be arduous, getting down to it, and there is no cable long enough to haul it up. John has come to terms with the idea of J.R. enfolded in his truck, how that steel crypt will serve as his monument. Much more than a headstone, it will mark his fortitude, his passage. Now there are two who John loved taken by the mountain.

He estimates he will attain fifty miles an hour by the time

he collides into the quad cab broadside. And as he hears the rumble of the pickup nearing, he toes the tachometer up to 3000. The impact will be of crushing proportions, but he is well braced in the three-point belt and with the energy absorbed by the v-blade and the front end of the wrecker, he might even come out of it in one piece. It is just possible John Ainsworth will live this one out, be thanked for his courage, say his goodbyes in a proper way, leave quietly to pass away in peace.

The quad-cab moves into view. It is monstrous, sheeted in steel, a clumsy abomination on its way to assault John Ainsworth's household, everything inside it, which is not going to happen, not even close, as John releases the brakes against the straining engine and the International, if not exactly leaping, does bull forward at a good rate, with the armored pickup moving into trajectory and the wrecker's diesel furiously clattering, the trees, the ground, sliding past, the wedged blade centering on the target out ahead, closing on the armor welded to the driver's door.

The impact is astounding, the rent of iron, the explosive caving in of bulk, everything in front of John folding up, smoke and glass and shredded metal rippling the air, the side of the quad cab punching inward and the truck itself heaved off its tires, groaning onto its side, a wounded elephant.

John wrests his wheel, the wrecker skidding sideways.

He has time to watch the quad-cab complete a roll-over and come shuddering to rest back onto its tires. His International stops sliding and John is out his door, 30-30 in hand. He hasn't run much of anywhere in the past few years, but he is running now, full tilt, advancing on the ruined pickup, dust and debris floating. He halts at the driver's side, taking aim, dizzy from the exertion, his balance faltering, his bearings loose, spinning, and then the spinning stops. The half of the quad cab that John faces is an oily mass of contorted iron and steel and the reek of fuel is thick. Gas seeps freely from the underside and John Ainsworth retreats, a flaming commencing from within the torn metal.

He is at safe distance when the gas vapor choking the air ignites with a thundering boom. The blast rocks the truck and fire tongues out from gaps in the twisted welded panels and in crossing the front of the truck John sees that the passenger door has jarred open. Gaseous particles sear him, the fire and smoke make confirmation difficult. He can see within the jagged convolutions of metal and plastic a piece of bent dashboard, a glimpse of steering wheel folded on itself. The driver would be clamped in those jaws.

Heat and flames roar. John backs away. He scans the field, the trees, the roadway, and picks up where the snowmelt bears boot tracks winding into the brush. Wade had cohorts. This one has survived and is on the loose.

The snowfall is a silent shower. Winchester in hand, John treads through the fluttering whiteness stalking the quarry. The quad cab is falling behind him, engulfed, a red and black inferno, and this gives him strength. He has become the hunter, following sign, the grids of boot soles, the fresh spore of blood.

The man is wounded, weaving across the ground, his trail proves it, and as John moves toward a stand of sedge, he knows the tracks will end here. His rifle barrel parts the spiky brown flowers and Bob Gates, on his side in the stems, expires in that moment. He gasps, teeth bared, head torn open, left arm shattered and hanging bloody. His eyes stare up at John Ainsworth and the glint of white sky captured in them fades, leaving two dim sightless orbs. John is grim, looking on him. The snow sifts down, flakes filling the dead man's bearded mouth.

John turns for home. Rayann will have barricaded herself in the house and he will join her there. He is injured, dragging, but he celebrates inwardly. Wade Deal and his ilk are at last vanquished. Cope and its people will pick up the pieces. They will go on, and John hopes for their sake it will be in a new way.

Snow drifts, the shadows of day's end lengthening.

John Ainsworth, melting into the dusk, becomes a shadow himself.

Chapter 41

Cole Cantwell arrives in Cope in the twilight, the tanker truck that conveyed him parked near the pumps of the gas station. With all the destruction, the mood is bleak, but the Propane Man is seeing his deliveries through, stacking gas cylinders, the survivors will need them. Cole has more pressing matters at hand, searching the office, the garage, the lot, seeking Rayann, her father.

The front window glass is webbed, holes blown through, the walls are riddled. He sweeps out of the building, passing the gaping window frame of the Cope Café, and now he is sprinting. He has no weapon, only his will, his fearsome desire to lay eyes on her, to secure her. His boots pound the pavement. Ainsworth's bungalow is less than a mile, and still he might be overdue.

The church comes up on his right, the smoking remains of it, charcoaled beams, red-eyed cinders, and an apparition standing over them. As Cole nears, the Pastor turns his way. He says nothing, his eyes like holes, his face stripped of blood, heat, any recognition of who he looks on. He is lost, or maybe by the terms of who he serves, he is found. Cole must forge on, keep his stride, make the distance.

He is in an-all-or-nothing mode, has undertaken a contract, he is striving to make good on an unspoken pledge. More than a feat on the slopes, a leap off the cliff face, it's an emergence, a fusion to greater substance. Rayann is a beacon, guiding him. In her cause, in reuniting with her, he hopes to transcend the limits of himself.

Dusk boils redly, apocalypse tinting the air. The wreckage is dead ahead – Ainsworth's tow truck, the blackened hulk of another vehicle. Nearing, Cole understands that the smoking ruin is Wade Deal's quad cab, and the twisted snow plow on the front end of the tow truck is what crushed it. He doesn't know whether Rayann or her father was behind the wrecker's wheel, either of them could have led that attack. He slows, moving past. There is no one, friend or enemy, present.

Lungs rasping, he picks up his pace.

*

Rayann has overloaded. She stalks the living room, her worries for her father, her apprehension for Cole, tearing at her. The din of warfare rang for an hour, gun fire, bomb-like blasts, the metallic explosion of a collision. The clamor advanced, growing louder, and then silence. Tension building, the unknown hovering, she orders the boy to stay put and flings open the front door.

She bears the rifle. From the porch she searches the swirling dimness, frantic to catch sight of either man. Smoke spills upward from someplace beyond her sightline. She thinks the chances slim someone could walk out from such destruction. The minutes crawl, her eyes cutting the night.

From the stillness, an unsteady gait treading snow. Rayann readies the gun. A shape comes forth from the gloom.

She leaps from the porch, her shoes slipping over icy footing as she dashes out to meet her father.

He is halting, worn to bone, his life force draining. He takes her in his arms, then she is leading him up the porch, into the barricade, the door bolted, locking out the night. She secures her father and John Ainsworth slumps into his chair, the woodstove light warming his gaunt features.

Ty keeps his distance. His senses are pitched, he is waiting for the battle he heard outside to resolve itself. By his expression, he has already chosen sides.

"They're out of business," John tells everyone. "I came into them hard and they did not survive it."

Rayann hugs him tightly. He is no braggart, just stating facts, terminal, mortally tired, and never more heroic.

Her father studies her. "Cole?"

Her eyes hold certainty. "He's on his way."

John Ainsworth nods.

"I believe in you, daughter. If not much else."

She says, "Cole will come back, dad."

Ty has retreated. He leans into the plywood sheeting a rear

window, his eye against the hole drilled for a gun port.

"He's here."

Rayann, her father, go still. They stare across to the boy and he stares back solidly, not allowing them to read his thoughts.

Rayann's pulse skips.

"Well, let him in."

Her son obeys, freeing the back door.

It hinges open and what Rayann sees first is the tactical vest weighted with magazines, an assault rifle braced in two gloved fists, and her thought is that Cole has so equipped himself and the thought dies as the man in the black knit cap comes into focus.

Wade Deal's gaze repels light, crossing Rayann, settling on her father.

"He's a goddamn zombie," John utters.

Wade enlightens him. "Bob had the wheel."

John does not stir.

"Bob took the brunt of it," Wade Deal says, stepping inside, not greeting his son. Oxidized blood stains the side of his face. His weapon is angled into the room.

"I hauled him out," Deal says. "Threw him on my shoulder. He pleaded for me to set him down and move on... Which I did."

Wade's rifle sights float toward Ainsworth's chest. "Bob Gates, he knew the ropes..."

John watches from his chair. His Winchester leans near the stove, within reach.

Rayann, breath rapid, grips her own rifle. Held crosswise to her, it will take speed and accuracy to swing it to the target in time.

"Good man, Bob." Wade says. "But you got to keep pace."

John snatches the Winchester, Rayann's rifle barrel arcing onto Wade, who fires at the same time, the burst from his assault weapon spitting into her father, the Winchester still inches away.

Ainsworth is driven into the upholstery of the chair, Wade already across the room, his rifle butt cracking into Rayann's jaw. She drops instantly.

"Like a trap door opened under her," he says.

He takes a moment to check his vest, the new gunshot hole in one magazine pouch. He withdraws the dented magazine inside it and tosses it over his shoulder. It lands near the boy.

Deal observes John Ainsworth, head pitched back, shirtfront sodden with blood. He delivers a memorial.

"Quicker this way, John."

He turns to Ty, gaping, paralyzed.

"Gonna make yourself useful?"

Ty beholds the demon that is his father.

"How?" he manages.

Wade's forbearance is nil.

"Get your mother's Jeep. Bring it around front."

The boy nods sharply. "Yes, sir."

"Don't sir me, short dog. This ain't the fuckin military. It's a pack of maneaters, extreme in its savagery. You gonna keep pace, or do I have to leave you behind like poor Bob?"

Ty, quaking, exhilarated, ventures a proud answer. *"You'll have to keep pace with me."*

Wade eyes him for several moments.

"Brash," he intones.

Then he grins. A terrible grin it is.

Chapter 42

Cole's lungs slam as he closes in on the rim of light, the flare in the night he has been pursuing. The Ainsworth's bungalow is emerging from the darkness, the fixture on the porch burning a halo through the frost. The front door stands open.

Boots crushing into the slush, Cole jumps across tire tracks scoring the driveway and narrowing up the road. What he has been dreading is already before him. Rayann's Jeep is missing and when he bounds up the porch, bursting through the doorway, the first thing he sees is blood spattering the hardwood floor.

John Ainsworth occupies his favored chair with a tangible permanence, a reverberating stillness. His chest is frayed, his head flung back. His eyes are visible in their seams, fogged, severed from the person that inhabited them. Cole grieves for Ainsworth, for what has been lifted from him. Only the husk remains.

He never got to his Winchester. The trophy rifle, blue steel, brown walnut, has been overlooked, because it remains where Cole surmises Rayann dropped it. He takes it from the floor and slides the breech open and sees and smells that it has been fired. Only once, because the magazine he ejects and snaps back in place still holds three rounds.

Not long afterward, a far-off wail floats to him.

Sprinting back to the gas station, Cole stops and turns. His eyes fix on the black mountain looming over Cope. The howling issues from the plateau, he visualizes Wade Deal's jaws flung open, his corded throat.

In the shattered office Cole tears through drawers, seizing a handful of labeled keys. Roving the yard, he matches keys to a mid-sixties sedan. Crusty with rust and upholstered in moss, it starts up after a long, slow crank. It lacks urge, the shifter is balky, but it does find its way to the road, the rear wheels spinning freely when the surface gets mushy.

Deal has announced himself, roared his beastial claim on the fallen village, on Rayann, her father, the boy. He has no notion that his adversary has survived the crevasse and is just below, in pursuit.

The advantage is Cole's. When he surprises Wade he will be three rounds ahead of him.

*

He alights from the sedan short of the plateau, cutting the engine and lights and leaving the car on the side of the road. The remaining distance he covers with rifle in hand.

A powdery flurry spills, muffling the sound of his approach. He passes Rayann's Jeep, slewed into a drift, abandoned. Dim light leaks from the seams of the massive doors built into the rock. The doors are closed but the locking mechanism is not engaged. Cole takes a handhold, applies strength, edging one door open. When he has enough width he slides through.

He stands at the portal of carved rock, the glimmer from overhead lamps undulating. The tunnel recedes, ancient timbers sagging as though weary of holding the roof up.

The atmosphere is weighted, acrid with the exhalations of decomposing sulfides. He hears nothing. Sound dies before it can travel far. His progress through the dank passageway is aided by his penlight, its beam grazing tortured folds of metamorphic rock, piercing the ochre internals of the mountain. The floor is deep with dust, sharp with broken quartz.

He begins passing artifacts, things left behind eighty years ago by miners focused on returning to daylight, breathable air.

His light picks up the beaten metal of an oil can. Further in, it glances off goggles, the lenses opaque. Then a shovel. A Prince Albert tobacco tin. Rounding a bend, he lights up an ore cart tilting on broken rail track. Past that, a great hole in the tunnel wall.

Cole arrives before it. It is a crosscut, an intersecting passage with an entrance much wider and taller than he is. He is not planning to enter until he sees the grooves in the dirt at his feet. A closer look reveals the impressions of tire treads.

He throws his beam within. It falls short of something large occupying the crosscut, a hulk that assumes shape and color as he moves toward it. The color is orange, the shape is a pickup, burly, high off the ground. His light touches the rear of the cab, illuminates the vacant rack in the rear window.

Cole has identified the truck. He wields the rifle that hung in the rack. The two would-be hunters he does not mourn. He imagines they lie with their sternums cleaved under the thin soil of a nameless draw and that is their only memorial.

He can make out other shapes in the tunnel ahead, he feels an outflow from that direction, a current of decay.

He moves on, his light streaming over a haphazard stack of skis, some of wood, a rusty kerosene stove, a discarded backpack, and he recognizes what he has walked into. The hidden history of Cope molders here. The horror show part.

The crosscut is a junkyard, a graveyard. Over the years the property of the dead has been randomly entombed.

He draws near a convertible from the 60s, layered with dust, tires flat. On the front seat, an open suitcase, old garments spilling from it, a paperback, a hairbrush.

Moving past a snowmobile, an early model, he pauses to study the holes punched in the metal, the streaks splashed across it that look like old blood. He can hear his lungs working, short, hard bursts, the oxygen is narrow here, or he is breathless. He has walked onto sacred ground, intruded on the personal leavings of past lives. A chamber of private discards awaits him, a collection of materials linked to humans, all of it broken, wearing away.

He starts forth. The fetid smell of ruin saturates the gloom.

Old clothing, stiff shoes, piled high.

The skeleton of a Model T.

He brightens an apparition. A buggy with a rotting top and tall spidery wheels.

As Rayann said, it goes all the way back.

His light sweeps a card table, the surface cluttered with the ephemera of those who once were. Cheap jewelry, emptied wallets, looted purses. A handful of scattered drivers' licenses.

He peers down at the yellowed, rotting cards. The dates start in the late 50s and climb the decades. The images that haven't been obliterated by time are all males. Men of their respective eras regard the camera in front of them, none with an inkling they will one day drive up the mountain and never drive back down.

A faint clanging commences.

Cole trains his ears, seeking the direction of the sound.

Leaving behind the ghostly chamber, he strides from the crosscut and into the main tunnel.

The clanging has more volume, a muted metal ringing from deeper into the mountain.

He hefts the rifle. Deeper he goes.

Chapter 43

The mine elevator at the dim end of a corridor has been immobile in its shaft for a century, suspension cable bound, the great drum that raised and lowered it frozen far above. The elevator car is framed by cage work. Miners crowded into it to descend and ascend hundreds of feet. The bars framing the cage are scabrous, over every surface corrosion blooms, eating away the steel.

A chain and padlock prevent the barred doors from opening. Effectively, the elevator is a cell. It contains a single prisoner. Her eyes show whitely, she is behind the bars, an iron spike gripped in her hand. The spike strikes the metal with a clash that resonates outward, lost in the tunnels beyond.

Rayann is streaked with grease and dust, a purple welt where Wade's weapon struck mars her jawline. Her hair is dirty and strung across her face, she is worn down, but she hasn't given up on the idea that she will be rescued. That Cole Cantwell is alive and will somehow make his way to her.

*

He doesn't like the noise. His head throbs and his neck is wrenched, probably from the impact of the collision, and just generally he is disgusted with the direction things have taken. He is thinking that if she doesn't stop that fucking banging he's going to stalk in there and snap her neck. The only thing that stops him is a better plan he has for her. It is simple, it is perfect, and she is deserving of that fate.

Lit starkly by lantern, Wade Deal is seated on a dusty crate under the arched ceiling of a cavern he calls his bunker. The boy sits on his own crate across from him and looks on as Wade assembles a sort of supper. He rips open a pair of MRE bags and slides the packaged contents onto the cable reel that serves as a table between them. "Beef stew," he explains, opening pouches. "Rice. Peanut butter. Fruit of some sort." He tosses the heater bags designed to cook the meal without fire, empties the food packets onto two metal plates. He thumbnails a matchstick, ignites the tip on a propane canister.

"Grunt chow," he tells the boy. "Soldiers serving as slaves to the government have to eat it." He passes the jet of the torch over the plates, smoke curling. "I keep it on hand for lean times, of which this is one." Sliding a plastic spoon across to the boy, he shovels a mouthful of warm brown glop.

Ty follows his example, finding the meal better than it looks. "Why the lean times, Wade?" He scans the assorted equipment and supplies stockpiled around them. "Looks like we got enough stuff here to get through anything."

Wade savages his food. "What would a chunky grub like yourself know about gettin through anything? You ever undergone privation? True hardship? With your belly shrunk against your spine and a blizzard at your back?"

Ty's plastic spoon falters. "Not exactly. But I ain't afraid to do it. I'm no crybaby. I never cry. You won't catch me doin that."

"We'll see about that, little man."

They fall silent, chewing.

The clanging comes to them, remote, the hollow bang of metal. The boy peers off into the dark.

"How long she gonna stay locked up, Wade?"

Wade rises from his seat, his plate cleared.

"Not much longer. Then you'll spill your tears."

Ty regards him, features tight.

"You gonna harm her?"

"It'll be quick."

"I ain't party to that."

Ty's father retrieves his tactical vest from a peg. "You're party to me. And I everything I say and do. That's how it lays out."

The boy is jarred by an unsettling perception.

"You think they'll be coming for you soon?"

Wade stabs himself into the vest. "I think I'm a dire wolf. A high country prince of darkness. Half carnivore, half ghost. They'll never catch sight of me. Until its too late."

Ty stares up at him. In the throb of the lantern, his father's eyes are hollows in his skull.

"Got that right," the boy says, forcing some life into his tone. "You are way ahead of them."

"So far out front I'm comin in from behind."

"They don't have a chance in hell."

Wade's caved gaze locks on him.

"You playin up to me?"

Ty is very still.

"No, sir."

"What'd I tell you about *sir*."

"Not to say it."

His father breathes out a growl. He picks up his assault rifle, slings the strap over his shoulder.

"Learn this: We share genetics with the lupine. Outlaw flesh eaters, fully armed. A hybrid pack of two. I'm the progenitor, you're the pup. Our range is a thousand square miles."

The boy conjures an endless land of granite.

"We stake out territory, son. We track. We lie in wait. We claw down prey." He strides to Ty, bids him stand.

The boy rises, encompassing the force that is his father.

"I will educate you. I will mend you when you are injured. In times of hunger, you will eat first."

Their gaze meshes, a charge infusing each.

"I will love you. You will know family."

Ty is speechless, enthralled.

Wade says, "You party to that?"

The lantern strobes, the rock of the cavern soaring around them. The boy wants to make an avowal, searches for the words.

"He is not."

The voice is deep, strong, certain. It stills them. They turn.

He emerges from shadow, the light of the lantern trenching the crags of his face. Macchus Deal stomps forth, his width and breadth consuming the space he moves through.

He halts, surveys the man and the boy, hands buried in the pockets of his rough jacket.

They take some moments to adjust to him.

"Bad news on the hoof," Wade says.

His father looks on him gravely.

"Three generations. May the child be spared."

Wade scorns the sentiment.

"What brings you here, old lion?"

Macchus Deal's answer is direct. "My life has brought me here. The wrong roads taken. The undying regrets." He measures his son. "I turned you into what you are. I'm here for a reckoning."

Wade watches his father's hands, hidden in the jacket.

He says, "How you intend to go about it?"

Macchus withdraws a flashlight from one pocket, flicks the beam onto a stack of wooden boxes. They are from an earlier time. They are labeled: Hercules Powder Company

"The Zelda mine goes," he says. "And everything in it."

Wade's eyes narrow on the explosives.

"That shit won't light. It's fifty fuckin years old. Nitro's all sweated out."

Macchus nods toward the tunnel. "I brought fresh dynamite. It's all in place. Situated to bring the mine down."

The clanging from the recesses resumes.

Macchus bends an ear toward it.

"Got the woman back there," Wade tells him. "The boy here. Gonna blow them up?"

"Release them."

Ty steps forth. He is awed by his grandfather, his enormity, but he has a declaration.

"I'm with Wade, grandpa."

Wade slants his eyes to him. Pleased.

Macchus sighs. "You're a green shoot. You have a lifetime ahead to make your mistakes. Don't let this be the worst of them."

The boy blinks, feeling the weight of his words.

"Wish I'd had your learned council," Wade says. "Way back when. Might have viewed things a little differently. Hog-roped to a fencepost kind of addled me."

His father's face is etched with grief.

"I've lived with that," he says. "It has darkened each day. If you atone, if you cast out the devil that drives you, I will clasp you to me as my blood once again."

For long moments, Wade Deal stands stricken, his natal past reaching toward him, the primal needs of sons for fathers, what he killed and buried threatening to unearth. But the image of a whipped boy beseeching God in a freezing black field interferes. It inflames him, flames that fill his eyes, the memory and all else slides away.

The pistol holstered in his vest is now in his hand.

Macchus' visage, the cliff of his face, shows no reaction, the aim of his eyes steadied on his son.

"Cast the devil out?" Wade says. "The devil living in your heart, that came out through your whip hand? Horned motherfucker jumped inside my ribcage and he's been scrambling around in there ever since. Man, I tell you, it's been one blighted trail."

"That trail ends here."

They behold each other, what is left of them.

Wade says, "Not for me."

The blast rocks the cavern, the boy's scream erased by the detonation bursting from the barrel of Wade's firearm. Macchus does not reel back, he absorbs the impact, never removes his eyes from Wade's deed.

"How's that feel?" Wade snarls. *"Father. Daddy."*
Enraged, he pulls the trigger again, and this time something is cut in the mass of his father. Macchus staggers, stepping away, his great back slamming against the rock of the cavern wall.

Wade, unrepentant, the boy aghast, watch him lose his legs, slide down the wall to the dirt. He is still, his torso upright, but the light in his eyes does not leave.

"You killed grandpa," Ty shrieks. *"You killed my grandpa."*

Wade, past all limits, glares on his son.

"Say some words over him. I have more killing in mind."

And he is gone.

Chapter 44

She is ready for him when his shadow crosses the cage. He has a light in one hand, the other keying the padlock, and when the chain drops and he hauls open the screeching door, she jabs out with the spike in her fist and the rusted end of it digs into his face. It gouges into his cheekbone, she was aiming for his eye, and he bellows and backhands her. The blow takes her down.

She has fallen outside the cage. Wade launches his boot into her side and she is jarred. He pockets the light, seizes her, hauls her up from the dirt. Heaving her over his shoulder, he treads along the striations of the tunnel.

Rayann is conscious, carried like a roll of carpet, her legs pinned by his arm, *"Put me the fuck down. Bastard son of a bitch."*

"We have a destination," Wade grunts. "When we arrive we'll fill our contract."

"You're out of your fucking mind."

He strides into the darkness with her.

"Never seen things more clearly."

They are consumed by gloom, his boots kicking splintered rock, splashing through pools of contaminated drainage. He rounds a curve and a kerosene lantern showers yellow light. It is hung from the ceiling and below it is a square hole in the dirt of the floor.

"Here we go," Wade says.

Rayann's head hangs behind him, he turns and the mouth of the shaft opens below her. She gapes at the timbered shoring that drops into the black of the earth.

Her tone is urgent. "Give it up. You do this, they'll stick a needle in your brain, put you in a fucking institution. The law is on the way..." The entrails of the earth breathe out, the malodor of the humid, endless deep.

"They'll find your... museum," she gasps. "The world will know. There's no place to hide."

Wade adjusts her weight on his shoulder.

"Let me go, Wade."

"That is the plan."

His arm, ridged with muscle, wraps her legs. "I could heave you over this way…"

Rayann recoils as the square hole shifts directly under her. Then she is slung up and over Wade's shoulder. She screams out, ends up half on her feet, crushed against his chest.

"But I want to see your face."

He has a handful of her hair. She fights, fastened tightly.

He turns with her toward the shaft.

"You'll have time on the way down to review how you've wronged me. Never did find the bottom."

With overpowering brawn, her offers her to the void.

A shout reverberates, jolting him.

"You're dead in my sights!"

Wade spins with Rayann locked to him. They both stare into the tunnel and Cole Cantwell walks into the edge of the lantern light. He braces the rifle against his shoulder, his eye to the scope and the barrel leveled.

Wade Deal shakes his shaggy head, his fist gathered in the woman's hair.

"You," he says.

"None other."

"Left you for dead and here you are back at me."

"Shoot him, Cole!" Rayann shouts. *"Don't fuss about me."*

Cole's hatred spikes, his finger tightens on the trigger. Wade Deal's head is the crosshairs, then he raises Rayann higher against him and it is no longer a viable shot.

"You know it's all over, right?" Cole says.

Wade's eyes flare from his torn face. He gauges everything, Cole's aim, his resolve, the trajectory. His shield is the woman and the moment she is not it will all break loose. He can easily restrain her with one arm while the other hand fronts the pistol, twelve in the magazine and all headed the flatlander's way. He can beat that rifle with a well-placed fusillade.

"I dispute what you said," he tells Cole. "This thing we

have, it's a goin concern. Average out a few lost souls against a century and a half, it doesn't make a dent."

Cole tracks him through the scope.

"This thing we have? We? It's down to you and a child."

Wade grips his semi-auto, slipped from his vest and jammed behind Rayann's back. He watches Cole's rifle, the black bore of it.

Rayann squirms, eyes cocked downward. "Shoot him, Cole! Shoot him *now!* He's got a gun!"

Cole exhales, sweat sliding down his ribs. There is no shot, there is not enough target.

"It's like this," Wade tells Cole. "You eat your enemy. You get renewed. People have, always will, go missin every day."

With all her strength, Rayann wrenches against his arm and he has had enough, flinging her off her feet with one mighty swing and opening fire on Cole.

Rayann, whipped back, drops into the mouth of the shaft.

She vanishes before Cole's eyes. Stricken, lead zipping past him, rock chips flying, he is immobilized until a round smacks into his thigh, and then he snaps his eye to the scope. The rifle kicks into his shoulder, muzzle flaming.

Wade's storm of gunfire ceases.

He feels for a wound and his finger slips into the puncture in the flat of his face. A shot cracks and a second puncture appears in his forehead, a piece of his skull at the rear blowing out.

His eyes roll up, he sways, steps blindly into the shaft.

Cole drops his smoking rifle, dashing along the tunnel. He skids to the edge of the square hole, the last of his adversary a tiny blur, then gone, like a match that goes out.

He is not there to cancel out Wade Deal, he is searching the shoring for some sign of Rayann.

"Here, Cole!"

She hangs by her arms from a crosspiece not ten feet down. Her feet dangle, her breath comes fast, her eyes widening as Cole slides into the shaft, grabbing onto a crosspiece and starting his way down. He is sure in his movements, has never been surer, and he can see from above that her grip on the wood is loosening.

The drift of decay washes up, blunt in the nose, and with it a dim undertone rising, a moaning. The dead in the regions below glance through his mind, a subterranean stirring wafting up the torment of phantom souls.

Stepping onto the timbers below Rayann, Cole braces his arms against the posts. He looks up to her, her feet not far above.

"Release your grip," he directs. "Wrap your arms around my neck as you drop."

She angles her eyes down, hesitating.

"Go ahead," he says. "You're good."

"Better be," she mutters. "Got one shot."

She lets go, plunging, her arms seize his neck. Cole rocks, taking her weight.

"Okay," he groans. "We're out of here."

"I can climb."

"Keep those arms locked. Don't want to lose you."

He makes his way up the shoring with her clung to his back. He never steps wrong, his hands never slip as he grabs his way upward. They crest the top, and rising from the opening they spill onto the tunnel floor.

Rayann sobs, he himself sobs, embracing each other in the dust under the yellow lantern.

Cole faces her. "That was a trip."

"Leave without me next time."

And then they are laughing, delirious heedless laughter at their continued survival, at being together, at winning their place.

In all this he feels the gunshot for the first time.

She sits up. His pantleg is saturated, the round entering the meat of the thigh.

"How did you stay up?"

"Adrenalin."

He looks to Rayann's injuries "Can you walk?"

She is bruised but brazenly alive. "Can you?"

He nods. They stand. "This place is primed to blow," she says. "Can you run?"

Chapter 45

Ty stays with his grandfather, wrapping his wounds with burlap torn from empty bags. The old man's guts are trussed and he is bleeding but he has gotten to his feet and together they head down the tunnel and toward the doors to the mine.

"I heard them shooting," the boy says.

"A pitched battle. Wade ran into someone."

"Did the law come in?"

"I'm guessing not."

"Then who?"

Macchus halts, trying to withstand the rip of his insides. He nods ahead and they watch the tunnel.

Rayann comes jogging from the shadows, Cole just behind her, lame on one leg. Violence has blasted them both.

She stops, distressed on seeing Macchus.

"Dad. You need a doctor."

Macchus takes in her injuries.

"Look to yourself, young lady."

The boy does not go to his mother. He reads Cole's face.

"Is Wade dead?"

Cole blinks slowly. He is tired. Tired of the boy. Tired of the way of death on the mountain.

"If he isn't," he says, "He's got a long climb up."

Ty's eyes sharpen, eyes beyond his years. His father's eyes.

Rayann dwells on her son, not of her anymore, thrall to some dark and bloody ritual his sire spawned.

Macchus finds a low ledge of rock and lowers himself onto it. He is breathing harshly, removes from his jacket a square device.

"Detonator. You have eight minutes to clear the mine."

The electronics are engulfed by his hand. On the digital read-out the seconds flash by.

Rayann starts toward Macchus, Cole holding her back.

She appeals to him. "Come with us."

Macchus rests on the ledge, he is part of the ledge, such is his makeup, the unyielding surfaces that comprise him. He looks on Rayann. They both know he is not leaving.

Macchus says, "I tried absolution and it fired back into me. We'll not know the grace of forgiveness. Not father. Not son."

Cole nods to Rayann. Time is short. Distressed, she gathers the boy, grips his unwilling hand.

Ty challenges Macchus.

"You just gonna sit there? Let the mine bury you?

In answer, his grandfather raises the detonator, displays the digits quickly expiring.

"Make haste, boy. I joined the darkness a long time ago."

*

Planting the charges, he had concentrated on the mine's first level, the workings that would bring down untold tons of rock and dirt and seal the deeper reaches, the adits and shafts, the crosscuts and winzes. Straight dynamite would do the job, at 60% nitroglycerin. The bundled sticks were embedded at the prop timbers of roof supports, in boreholes, key structural points that on signal would violently give way.

His remote is radio controlled and the sequence of detonation is already triggered. He contemplates the ruin of his domain, how with hammer and chisel he has struck his way through life, never giving clemency, never extending charity, or the roots of humankind. He thinks about his wife of sixty years and what he told her before he left. That thereafter she would assume the reins, steel herself and conduct her way through the remainder of her life alone. He left her money he'd hoarded, a ten-inch stack of cash so that she would not go without. He remembers her face then, how before him the flesh withered and her eyes turned to dark colored glass. She held herself tightly, not flinching at the words that lacerated her, and walked into the kitchen. He saw her shadow cast on the floor, standing at the sink for long minutes and what was left of his shriveled heart was squeezed away.

His time is at hand.

One second becomes zero and a pulse finds its wavelength, the current firing along the braided electric cables that fuse the bundled cylinders of nitroglycerin packed in diatomaceous earth. The blasting caps ignite and the shockwave is unimaginable, the velocity of it, the sear of superheated gas. The roof and walls shatter and in the crushing instant left to him he faces a blizzard of flyrock and is rocketed to the gates of a fiery portal.

It does not open on any form of God.

*

Rayann drives, the Jeep curving down the mountain road, the pines blinking by. She has gathered speed because Cole is hurting, his leg wound seeping through the improvised dressing knotted around his thigh. The boy is in the back, head turned to granite peaks fracturing pale sky.

A boom quakes, rolling.

They never see the blast, only feel the air shudder.

"So ends the saga," Cole says.

Rayann flinches at her harrowed reflection in the mirror.

"Paid a high price."

"Almost everything."

Their eyes meet.

Ty's voice cuts in from behind them.

"It didn't end."

They glance at him.

"It's just beginning."

*

The waiting room of the hospital in the valley is vacant except for Rayann and the boy. A lamp glows on an end table, he is dead-out on some seating, she is in a chair. She has changed her clothes, her injuries have been tended. Long hours have passed. She is half-lidded, watching the sun cresting the trees beyond the parking lot.

A surgeon comes out to talk to her. He looks to have missed as much sleep as she has, tells her he removed the majority of the bullet from the soft tissue of Cole's thigh. Some fragments he couldn't remove without doing more damage, they will form scar tissue and become part of Cole's leg. Lead from a gun comes in hot, burns a pathway. He's treating local infection with antibiotics. There may be some nerve damage. The good news is the bullet missed the femoral and other bleed-out arteries. Cole will likely have a limp.

When Rayann goes to Cole's room a sheriff's deputy is on his way out. She has already given him her statement and he nods to her in a friendly way. She smiles back, and her smile leaves her as she walks in and sees Cole attached to tubes and monitors, his leg heavily bandaged, grinning at her from his bed.

She heads straight for him, buries her face against his chest. He strokes her hair. She leans up.

"How are you?" she asks.

"Lines in, lines out. And you're healing fast."

They gaze on each other.

He says, "I've been thinking about us."

"What did you come up with?"

"That we might have a future."

She gauges him. "I got my work cut out for me."

He squints at her. "Are you talking about me?"

"You are a given. I'm talking about rebuildin. Folks are gonna need that gas station."

He shakes his head sadly. "Do you know what kind of a zoo Cope is gonna turn into? When the media grabs hold of what went down, what's been going on for decades, the public will flock to the mountain. They'll be crowding the street, hoping to sight backwoods cannibals. You'll have no peace."

"And the pumps will spin."

"That doesn't sound like you."

Her features are resolved.

"I'm staking my claim, Cole. I'm carryin forward what my father spent his life working for. I'm givin Ty a decent home, if he wants it. I will stay in Cope and I will tend John Ainsworth's grave."

He starts to interject, sees she won't be swayed.

She says, "I'd like you to be part of it."

Cole tries picturing that.

"That means a lot to me. That invitation. Not sure how much help I can be. A gimp running the nozzles. But I don't know. Did you ever see Gunsmoke? Chester had a pretty good limp there, and he got things done."

"Shut up, you big baby. You'll be back on your skis and I'll hardly see you."

"I'm at loss what to do in the summer."

"Take up flycasting. When the sheriff gives back that fancy rifle, supply us with venison."

A pall falls over them.

"The rifle's not mine. I don't think I could hold that rifle again. Or any gun."

She commiserates.

"Well. You'll be the odd man out, but that's what I love about you. Different drummer."

He takes her hands in his.

"You know, I have my own rebuilding coming up. It's down south. I have to tie up some loose ends. Square things. My mother needs me. She doesn't know it, but she does. And then…"

He trails off, looking into her eyes.

She leans down, her lips brush his.

"You know where to find me."

Rayann stands, walks to the doorway. She looks back at him, then she's lost to the corridor.

Cole stares after her. His leg hurts. His heart hurts.

"Don't think I won't."

Chapter 46

He buys a ticket to Pasadena and waits for the Greyhound in front of a market in downtown Bishop. The trip will take over nine hours and he will arrive in what is termed reduced circumstances. But he is still on the young side, fit and able, and he surprised everyone by how quickly he recovered the use of his leg. Psychological recovery is another matter, being shot exacts a host of posttraumatic stress reactions – anxiety, fear, horror and helplessness. All of which have visited him at various intervals, but in the main, he possesses a built-in mechanism that rights his outlook and keeps him afloat, and also helps remind him to stay humble.

Rayann had offered him the car from impound, it ran reliably enough to at least get him down there, but he didn't want to incur any debts. Getting things done on his own is crucial to taking charge of his life and its direction. He has enough money to live leanly but independently for the near future, and he will devise a continuance.

It took a transit bus to get to Bishop. From where he stands he can see the crags of Mt. Whitney to the south, and north up the range the heights of the mountain that shadowed the hamlet. There is snow on the peaks and he never did learn its name. No one in Cope called it anything but the mountain. That is what he'll call it.

It pulls on him, to gaze on the mountain from the distance of the valley floor. From here, it loses its size, its volume, and the time he lived under it is already dissolving. The bright, stirring days, the black terror, those events are stretching away.

What haunts him is not so much what happened up there, but what seems to be missing afterward. He has always skated through destinations unscathed. Strange that a hamlet called Cope is where he finally left something of himself behind.

What is missing is accounted for. It resides with Rayann.

The Greyhound glides up and the doors boost open. Cole shoulders his pack. What they went through rates a ballad, and he is the man to serenade her.

If only he could sing.

Chapter 47

John Ainsworth's bungalow proves sturdy, and by the summer, with a few helping hands, Rayann has repaired and reinstalled what was damaged. Currently, the house lofts woodsmoke from the chimney and inside glows with cleanliness and warmth. She runs a tight ship, even with her long hours at the gas station, but she has hired a man whose ranch went bust and he knows his way around machinery.

Her son Ty was not among the helpers putting things right. He is staying scarce, and that night Rayann has a premonition. In the mortal hours a howling comes to her, a ragged cry pitched from the reaches of the mountain. She knows who it is, she's been living with its wild frequencies her whole life, and those with lives before hers.

In the buttery cast of early morning, Rayann treads up the creaking stairwell fastening her robe. She steps onto the landing and pushes the door to the boy's room open.

He is not in there, and her premonition glares into life. The crossing over is complete, what has been taken from her is as vital as her own viscera.

She bore him, but the mountain is both mother and father.

She is shaken, her eyes fastened on the corner where he kept the wooden bow, the quiver of arrows.

She will be shaken again, when the rambler who left his heart with her comes striding up the road.

Chapter 48

The recurve bow, the quiver, the broadheads, are snugly positioned alongside his backpack and he is snowshoeing his way up the hard inclines of the alpine. The high slopes are melting, the sun sparkling like silver fairies off the ice. The sky is broad and blue, it is a fine day at elevation, cold, clear, and he is good with that. The terrible truths that live up here deserve their time in the light, where they can be seen for what they are.

Ty has no delusions about his own state of being, he is at last fully and gladly the boy-animal he knew himself to be. The beast that was his father walks ahead in his path, and the father of his father waits for them above, at the rim of the wilderness they will throw themselves into, a redoubt of fangs and blood.

The boy-animal halts, staring up to the carved white cliffs.

A howling greets him.

It raises the hair. Inspired, he plunges on.

*

His howl is an ancient message, a shrilling, a crazed song from the Pleistocene, when Canus Lupis first galloped through these trees. His howl is a territorial wailing, telling the land below who owns the land above. His howl is a jubilance, celebrating what stalks the hinterlands, and it is a mourning for what stalks the wilds no more.

He stands large, wrapped in skins, hawked features shaded by the mantle of his stitched hood. The smoke of his voice trails from his mouth, the bead of his eye locked on the slopes below.

Comes the boy, not far distant.

CPSIA information can be obtained
at www.ICGtesting.com
Printed in the USA
BVHW051045100223
658271BV00018B/729/J

9 798218 034702